Pelican Reach

A Novel of Frida Kahlo

Kenneth Kuenster

Pelican Reach

A Novel of Frida Kahlo

HISTRIA FICTION

Histria Fiction

Las Vegas ◊ Chicago ◊ Palm Beach

Published in the United States of America by
Histria Books
7181 N. Hualapai Way, Ste. 130-86
Las Vegas, NV 89166 USA
HistriaBooks.com

Histria Fiction is an imprint of Histria Books. Titles published under the imprints of Histria Books are distributed worldwide.

Library of Congress Control Number: 2024931069

ISBN 978-1-59211-455-9 (softbound)
ISBN 978-1-59211-469-6 (eBook)

One

A generation was skipped... this is what I conclude as I look into the mirror, with a photo of my mother on one side, and a photo of my grandmother Frida Kahlo on the other.

It's true my mother's eyebrows meet, and it's true she has slight fine hairs above her upper lip. But what's missing is the burning intensity that grandmother Kahlo and I share. It's in the eyes... I, like Kahlo, am unafraid to look at anything, and indeed have a lust to look at everything. And it's in the mouth... Frida's full lips are red with ripe opinions, as are mine.

And like Kahlo, most of my paintings are of myself... we are each our own muse.

It's not that I don't let other people into my life. It's often they who permit me my Frida-style self-scrutinizing... just as it was Diego Rivera, grandmother's husband, who provided her with her arena of self-observation... her sad and angry arena.

If you read a biography of Frida Kahlo, you'll find no mention of me or my mother.

Here is our history as I know it...

When Frida Kahlo was fourteen, still a school girl at the Preparatoria in Mexico City, and before the terrible accident on the bus that crushed her pelvis and caused other injuries that rendered her incapable of bearing children... when she was that child-woman, she met a Pamé Indian, a descendant of a long line of chiefs. He too was young, maybe eighteen or twenty. He was huge, had great girth. And he had a frog-like face. But Frida was inexplicably drawn to him... indeed obsessed by him.

They became lovers and met at odd times in the park.

Their sex was a ritual. He would lie on the ground and small delicate Frida would climb all over his mammoth body, provoking his senses and hers until she was held impaled and kissing his grotesque frog face.

How do I know this?

There is a diary of Frida's that was kept under lock and key by the Mexican government for forty years and then published in facsimile form, to much acclaim by art historians and Kahlo biographers.

There is no mention of Frida's frog liaison in that diary. However, there is another diary... kept over her younger years, starting when she was fourteen and which, like the later diary, is a beautiful meld of drawings and words.

I own this diary.

No one else knows it exists... at least that is what I believed until recently.

Two months ago, I received a letter addressed to the name I only use with friends as a joke, which makes the letter even more enigmatic...

**

Pelican Reach, California

13 March, 1997

Dear Frida Olhak,

I understand that you own an original Frida Kahlo manuscript, a journal of drawing and writing from her early years. Please forgive my intruding, but would it be possible for me to view this diary? I own several Kahlo self-portraits and they are among my favorite paintings in the collection here.

Honesty compels me to confess that I am very interested in purchasing this example of Kahlo's early work. But even if it is not available for purchase, it would give me great pleasure to view it.

I understand that for reasons of your own, the existence of the diary is not common knowledge. Indeed, I am one of only two people perhaps who know of its existence, now that your mother has passed away. Please accept my condolences on her passing.

Would you allow me the honor of viewing the diary?

I do so much hope to hear from you in the affirmative.

And you have my word that my knowledge of the existence of the diary will remain confidential.

Again, please forgive my intrusion.

Very truly yours,

Orlando Pettingill

P.S. Your surname fascinates me. Is it Mexican native...? Perhaps Pamé? And what a coincidence that your Christian name is the same as the creator of the work in your possession.

***

After I read the letter, I was haunted for days by the questions it raised...

How did this man discover the existence of the diary?

How did he locate me?

How did he know my mother died?

Is he really so naive that he doesn't see that the surname he used is the reverse spelling of Kahlo?

What does he know that prompts him to ask... is the surname native?

Who is this man?

***

Why is my existence a secret? Because my mother's existence was a secret from the moment of her conception. Frida was only fourteen when she became pregnant by the young fat Pamé chief, and though she was headstrong even then, she was confused about the baby growing inside of her. Grandmother Kahlo's father had Pamé blood in him, and it was decided that during her confinement, she would go to live with some Pamés on her father's side. When her baby (my mother) was born, Frida gave her over to the Pamés. Over the years Frida went to see my mother, who became more and more a Pamé in how she lived and thought. When, while still very young, my mother became pregnant while climbing all over some fat frog chief, I assume (I never knew who my father was), that event was kept from Frida, the Kahlo family, and Diego Rivera, to whom Frida was by then married.

Just before she died, Frida sent her youthful journal of drawings and writings to my mother, so my mother would know her origins.

I was raised among the Pamés, and our life was pleasant enough. Our descendants of chiefs had owned valuable land, so we were surprisingly affluent. It was that money that provided for my education, right up through the University of California, which I completed this year.

I liked growing up among women whose eyebrows met. I was also fascinated by the traditions and rituals of our people. For some ceremonies the women dyed their teeth blue.

They used to file them to a point, but only one woman in our village still had pointed teeth. She was over a hundred.

All the women had pierced nipples through which they wore fine white bones for those blue-teeth ceremonies.

When I reached puberty, my nipples too were pierced and, off and on since, I have worn the beautiful bones of a sacred Pamé hawk that was determined to be my spiritual companion. No non-native has ever seen my bone-pierced nipples, which are exotic and a little scary.

My one gringo lover, a tall, fair, affluent poet, looked carefully at my nipples, saw they were pierced, but was too wary to ask the purpose of the piercing.

***

Two months after I received the letter from Pelican Reach, the small studio I live and work in was broken into. Everything was carefully looked through. No damage was done and nothing was taken. I could only think that whoever it was, was after the Kahlo diary. Was it some agent of this Orlando guy... whose letter I never answered?

So I answered his letter...

***

Dear Orlando Pettingill:

My place was broken into and thoroughly searched. Since nothing was taken, I have concluded that whoever it was, was after Frida's diary (which I don't keep here).

Were you behind this?

Do you think that just because I ignored your letter, and because you have more money than God, you can just take whatever you want in life?

Yes, I do have Pamé blood in me... a lot of it... and I'm warning you that I also have Pamé power in me... too mystical for gringo comprehension... and if you persist in your pursuit of my precious Frida diary, I will use those powers!!!

Seriously,

Frida Olhak

***

A week later there was a knock on my studio door. I opened it to find a serious older man in a dark suit. He was holding a photo in his left hand, and under his right arm held a flat package wrapped in fine gray paper.

He looked at me, then at the photo, and spoke with a slight accent.

Ms. Frida Olhak...

He said this not as a question but as a statement. Please...

He handed me the package and turned to leave. It was unnerving.

Wait a second... who the fuck are you?

He turned, raised his eyebrows, and smiled slightly.

Please, I am but the messenger...

He moved silently down the stairs.

I stared at the package for a few moments, allowing my Pamé suspicions to surround it, and then cut through the dark blue twine.

I gasped.

I held in my hand a matted and framed very small drawing. It consisted of three female figures simply but beautifully drawn. They were standing alongside each other, the left figure the largest, the middle smaller, and the right figure quite small. They each wore simple Mexican dresses, and each had one continuous dark eyebrow. The only color was tiny bits of blue between the lips of the three figures.

It was signed... Frida.

Slipped into the frame on the back of the picture was a white envelope. I opened it and read the note...

My dear Frida Olhak:

I am so distressed.

It was certainly no one associated with me who broke into your studio, and it is so disconcerting to think that you would suspect me of such behavior.

Please accept this drawing as a gesture of my sincerity. It is one of a dozen or so of Kahlo's quick drawings that I own, and this one seemed especially appropriate for you. Even though it's well-known of course that Kahlo had no children, in this drawing she seems to depict herself with a daughter and seemingly a granddaughter. They are certainly all Frida's. Now, another matter ...again, please forgive my intrusion, but I've been told by someone whose judgement of painting I highly respect, that your own self-portraits are wonderful, unique works... Kahlolike, but with their own integrity. Which brings me to ask whether you might be interested in being a guest here at Pelican Reach.

I have enclosed directions. You may just appear any time. without prior notice.

Very truly yours,

Orlando Pettingill

P.S. I tried spelling your surname backward. I'm embarrassed by my density.

***

I sat and stared alternately at the drawing and at the note for a silent hour. How could he presume that I would just go to his home, not knowing him? Is he that determined to get his hands on my Frida diary? And who is it that's seen my paintings and said they're good? And that coy business about my name... does he know I'm Frida's granddaughter? Is that why he said this drawing was appropriate for me?

***

That night I went with friends to a small experimental theater in San Francisco to see some German performance artists. The performance ranged from pretentious to tedious, with generous doses of Germanic angst here and there. I realized once again how rarely the art of others interests me. However, there was one performer, a thirtyish blond woman, who fascinated me. She had neon blue eyes that shone with intelligence and defiance. Her pale blond hair was done in African dreadlocks. She was dressed in black, as was the whole troupe. But what was most striking was that she had hard red scars in the center of both palms and on both feet. Watching her as she assumed various positions, I saw that all of these scars went through and came out the other side. An image kept coming vaguely to my mind, but I couldn't place it.

Later I was at a party with these same Germans... my friends are theater people. The blond performer caught me staring a couple of times, and finally she stared hard at me and came over.

Frida Kahlo... she said.

What?

Frida Kahlo, she repeated, drawing it out as though I were dense. Then she ran a finger across my eyebrows saying, Frida, drawing it out even more, then Kahlo, she repeated as she lightly ran a fingertip over my trace of fine mustache.

Then, she smiled. We all have our marks, yes? She held her palms up before my eyes.

Her impertinence annoyed me.

You saw our performance, yes? What do you think?

I was bored.

I thought this comment would provoke her, but she shook her head and said softly, me too. I am leaving this group.

Then she smiled genuinely and said, don't be offended by my Frida comment... but the resemblance is amazing... you are surely her daughter, yes?

Granddaughter, I said, thinking, believe what you want.

I believe it, but most important, you are very beautiful, and you paint, yes. What is your name? I'm Hanna.

I shrugged my shoulders and said, Frida. Yes I paint. She laughed, yes, of course.

Hanna and I spent a couple of hours talking together midst the chaos of the party, and her severe shell soon relaxed. She was interested that I am a painter and that all my paintings are of myself.

One's self should always be the subject of one's art, she said.

At three or so in the morning she asked if she could stay at my studio... said that now that she's decided to leave the performance group she can't stand the idea of being with them one more night.

I was tired and a little stoned and I shrugged and said, okay.

But at my studio we did not sleep. Prompted by my asking about her scars, she sat up on my one mattress next to me and told me her bizarre story. The eeriest part was that she not only knows Orlando Pettingill, but has lived at Pelican Reach and has an eleven-year-old daughter who is still there. I was stunned, and combined with the drawing and letter from this Orlando, I wondered if my life was slipping into some psychic San Andreas rift.

Hanna has a fifth scar, a larger gnarled one in her right side, and when I saw it, I realize that the image that came to me earlier was of the stigmata of the Crucifixion, and I told her that. That's when she told me about her first performance piece in Germany, which she did with her twin brother, who is, disturbingly, the father of her daughter, and is now dead, a suicide.

The wounds (her brother had identical ones) she received escaping over the Berlin Wall from East to West, before the reunification of Germany.

The facts of her life are so unbelievable that at first, I thought she was making them up, that I had brought some deranged woman home. But by dawn, I believed it all... she was too convincing.

And at dawn, with the morning light slanting in on us from the tall windows. because of a question from her, I ended up telling her my life story.

Your nipples... they have piercings...

It was stuffy in the studio and we had both taken off our clothes.

Yes, that was done when I was twelve.

Hanna leaned over close to look, and said, they are openings for something to go through?

Yes, bird bones.

I explained the ritual and my Pamé heritage, and finally who my mother was... and my grandmother.

Hanna said, I thought that was true when we first talked, and when I saw your paintings tonight I knew it was true.

I showed her the white bones of the sacred hawk and she held them carefully and with intense interest.

May I put them in? She nodded toward my chest.

I was about to say no, that no one has ever done this but me, but I sensed that Hanna knew this.

I tipped my head down to contemplate it all. Finally, with my head still down I said, yes.

Hanna took hold of my right nipple with her thumb and finger and I pushed out my chest, watching.

You have to use a little saliva...

Hanna smeared a bit of spittle against my nipple with the finger of her other hand.

The bones are about three inches long and taper from a narrow point to about a quarter of an inch in diameter.

The thick end should be on the outside, I said, and they're meant to go in a little past half way.

Hanna nodded. Pulling my nipple out, she carefully inserted the narrow end, and twisting back and forth, gently pushed the bone in. Just before it was in the proper place, the opening stretched taut, which brought tears to my eyes as it always does.

Oh, does it hurt? Hanna asked in a whisper. We had both been holding our breath.

It's supposed to be a perfect balance between pleasure and pain.

And is it? Yes.

Hanna repeated the ritual on the other side, then sat back to admire her work.

Come here, she said, taking my hand and leading me to the large mirror that leans against the wall by my easel.

We stood side by side, studying ourselves.

I stood with my hands at my side, and with my breasts pushed out, as I always do when I wear my bones.

Hanna had her hands slightly forward, palms out, displaying her red stigmata scars.

We were the same height and the same build, but the similarity ended there. Hanna, with her citron dreadlocks and creamy skin, and I with my inky black hair and brown skin, were absolute opposites, and with that realization came caution. You'd better not betray me Hanna, I whispered menacingly.

Hanna had heard, and she turned quickly to look at me.

I rephrased my words... please keep my secrets, secret Hanna, and I will do the same with yours.

She was relieved and smiled.

We got back into bed and slept for ten hours.

***

Oh no, Orlando is a prince, you don't have to suspect him. Hanna and I were at an outdoor cafe, and I had told her about the strange recent series of events... the break-in, Orlando's letter, subsequent delivery of the drawing, and the invitation to Pelican Reach. I had brought the drawing with me, wrapped in its gray paper, because now I'm afraid to leave it in my studio.

Hanna asked to see it.

Oh, this is a jewel, and a real Frida! There you are, the three of you, but what is this blue business on the teeth?

I explained the Pamé tradition, and the powers that Pamé women have to deal with betrayal. I told her about my gringo lover, that he broke my heart, and so I broke his, and that only mine has mended, while his is underground.

Hanna asked what I meant, and I told her the story of my lover's wedding.

***

These were the words of the priest that day...

If any person present has reason to believe that these two people should not be joined as man and wife before God, make yourself known.

After he spoke, an absolute silence pervaded the gathering in the Basilica of the Carmel Mission, as the families and friends of my beautiful blond lover and his beautiful blond bride considered the absurdity of such an idea.

The silence, however, was invaded by an increasing rustle of formal attire as, one by one, people turned to look into the small chapel to the left of the nave.

There I stood, a still, solitary figure, young and dark.

Like a Kahlo self-portrait, I stared at the groom-to-be, and one over-sized tear, more like a crystal than liquid, welled in my left eye. When this tear dropped onto my left breast, over my heart, it formed a blood-red stain on my white Mexican wedding dress.

The groom-to-be put one hand out toward me, opened his mouth as though to call out, and collapsed. His tall beautiful body fell like a redwood against the bride-to-be, who in turn crashed into a covey of silly pink bridesmaids, sending them in all directions, one of whom struck the priest, whose bible sailed skyward, the black binding seen from the side mimicking the eyebrows that set it all off.

The wedding party was in a heap at the foot of the altar. The groom's large diamond cuff link (a gift from the in-laws-to-be) had snagged the bride's silk lacy bosom as he fell, tearing it open, exposing a pale breast. His face landed inches from her nipple, and still dazed, he murmured tenderly in Spanish/Indian and pursing his lips, he stretched to seek some nurturing.

The priest had recovered his bible, and eyeing the groom-to-be, brought the holy book down smart on the head of the would-be suckler.

The sound of the blow brought the congregation to its senses, and as one, the whole party turned noisily to look again into the small side chapel.

But I was not there, it was empty.

The wedding party circled the groom-to-be to see to his revival. But to no avail. He was dead.

They all looked up at the stern priest, who still held the bible. He stared at the shiny black weapon in his hand.

An autopsy later revealed the cause of death as heart failure. But I thought it was more like heart success. Mine.

That was in August of 1993.

***

When I finished telling my story, Hanna stared at me silently. She didn't know whether to believe me or not, but finally I could tell from her expression that she knew I'd told the truth about my Pamé power. But despite her bravura, she was unnerved.

Hanna then told me about her daughter at Pelican Reach... She is named Hans, after her father, my dead twin brother. She is a little not right in the head, because her father was my brother. I have not seen her in three years, and I have not missed her until recently. She has been happy there...

Orlando's servants take care of her.

Hanna said all of this coldly, in the way that she seemed when I first met her at the party.

***

The next morning, I had people to see at the university, and I left Hanna in the studio, asleep.

When I returned at noon. Hanna was gone. And so was the drawing.

I sat with my head on my arms in a mood of anger and sadness and stupidity, and finally anxiety as I raced across the room to the drawer where I keep my sacred bird bones... gone!

I was filled with Pamé rage. I will kill you Hanna.

***

Two days later, a small package arrived, and inside, carefully packed were the bones and a note... Even I could not keep these. H.

Two days after that, another package arrived containing the drawing. There was no note.

What a tormented soul, I think. But then, if I'd been perforated by East German bullets, and then penetrated by my twin brother, who afterward killed himself, to create a demented daughter whom I then left behind, I'd be tormented too.

The fact that Hanna returned what she took somewhat redeemed her in my eyes. After a few days, I found myself missing her.

***

A week later, there was another break-in and this time my things were gone through more roughly. I had begun to take my bones and the drawing with me whenever I went out so they were safe, and nothing else was taken.

It could have been Hanna, but I doubt it. It wasn't her style.

I sat silently for a few minutes, and then found my California map. Lying on the floor, I scanned the coast north of Mendocino. When I located Pelican Reach at the confluence of the Pelican River and the Pacific Ocean, I drew in a tiny round face with one dark-winged eyebrow above the eyes.

Two

Seeing him nude, you immediately think of a boy frog standing on his hind legs. His skin is greenish-white like that of an aquatic animal.

His large, dark and extremely intelligent bulging eyes, almost out of their orbits, are held in place with difficulty by eyelids that are swollen and protuberant, like those of a frog.

A huge corpulent frog.

Diego... my frog prince.

Frida Kahlo's diary, 1947

***

The taxi driver and I are stunned into silence as we stare at the shimmering apparition below.

He is a sweet alcoholic man of around fifty, whose breath gave him away as we drove out from town and he told me various stories about Orlando Pettingill. Stories told by people who had never laid eyes on the man or been on his estate.

And estate it is, starting with the black ornate iron gate we pulled open at my insistence (in spite of the sign reading ring and wait). But screw it, I thought, this man entered my life out of the blue and I will do the same to him.

The battered white cab is silent behind us and the driver and I stare down sixty feet below at eleven large pelicans swimming behind a great round pale green being with skinny legs rhythmically propelling itself frog-style beneath the surface of the clear river water.

We are interrupted by an icy foreign accent, Can I help you?

We turn to find a thin dark-haired man in overalls, a gardener it seems, who holds a pruning saw in one hand, but who wears a pistol in a holster on his hip.

I'm here at the invitation of Orlando Pettingill, I say defiantly.

We'll walk to the house, he says. Do you have any bags?

The driver hands him my duffle and nervously takes my money, anxious to be on his way before he forgets any of the details of the newest tale to be added to his repertoire.

The driveway curves away from the bluff above the river, through a grove of giant cypresses, and up onto a promontory overlooking the Pacific Ocean, which below is pouring its tidal power into the mouth of Pelican River.

Things happen here... that's the thought that floods my head.

We are walking up wide steps to a marble terrace that projects out from an immense ochre mansion. The gardener is in front of me with my shaggy canvas duffle slung over his shoulder, like an errant animal he's just shot with his pistol. At a side door he rings a bell and while we wait I watch twenty-foot swells roll in with such force it sounds like thunder.

The door is opened by a dwarf... no it's not a dwarf, it's a child with the aura of a small adult. Behind her is a Mexican maid, who fleetingly registers my own Mexicanes before assuming the role of servant expected of her. After a brief exchange with the gardener, she takes my bag from him and politely says in a strong Spanish accent, Please, you come this way?

The girl stands to one side. She has long robust blond hair and the same neon blue eyes as Hanna, and I realize she is Hanna's daughter. One leg is shorter and smaller than the other and she stands lopsided. A thin ribbon of drool hangs from her lower lip. She stares at me silently. As I am led down a corridor, the girl limps off to the right, down a smaller hallway.

After I've been shown my room by Marie the maid, I go off on a little exploratory expedition. I'm still thinking about what I saw from above the river... the pale green aquatic creature and its accompanying band of pelicans.

I find a winding path along the headlands starting at the mouth of the river, and follow it leading upstream as it gradually approaches water level. From about twenty feet away, concealed by shrubs, I watch a sudden eruption of the river produce the great green creature clambering up the bank, its flat webbed feet pushing vigorously to propel itself up out of the water. In its small dark green front foot it clutches the bunched-up neck of a shimmering balloon of fine netting quaking with the spastic activity of hundreds of small silver fish. The eleven pelicans are circling in front excitedly.

The green creature slaps a large flat foot against the surface of the river three times. Then there is silence as the pelicans, one by one, approach the bank of the river and the green creature reaches into the cavernous bill of each to deposit a few handfuls of flashing fish from the net in its lap. When all the birds have had their turn, they spread their huge primordial wings and one by one lift up from the water and fly downriver to the ocean.

The creature, after watching until the birds are out of sight, pulls off dark green gloves, and with small pale hands pulls off webbed rubber feet and a yellow-green cap. Then he stands and, reaching behind, pulls an outer skin down to reveal white flesh. The self-skinning continues, peeling green to free pale plump arms, shoulders, a soft breasty chest, great protruding belly, fat thighs, and skinny lower legs.

When he turns in my direction, his head is down but I can see enough of his face to know that I'm looking at Orlando Pettingill, because when I asked Hanna what he looked like, she said in her unsentimental manner, think of a fat frog.

He looks briefly in my direction, as though he senses another presence, but I know he cannot see me.

He is like a boy frog standing on his hind legs.

When he begins to gather up his wetsuit and gloves and flippers, I make my stealthy escape.

Agitated, I retreat up the path to the mansion, trying to sort out the tide of feelings coursing through me. My heart is pounding and I can't even begin to think through the whole pelican ritual.

What has taken me over is wave after wave of throbbing frog lust. Oh, Grandmother Kahlo, I am your granddaughter.

***

That evening, Marie and another, younger Mexican maid serve dinner to a small group of us, including Hanna's daughter, Hans, who stares at me unblinking and who sits immobile except to spoon in her food and occasionally wipe her mouth with the back of her hand.

There are two men in turbans who nod when I sit down but speak only to each other in Arabic.

A tiny, frail while-haired woman, elegantly dressed, introduces herself as Madame Pettingill, Orlando's mother. She keeps starting stories and then stopping abruptly, looking over at the window with a frown as though the rest of what she had to say has rudely flown from the room.

There are others in the mansion, because the younger maid comes three times from the kitchen carrying trays of food and heading off in various directions.

Later, as the sky held only the deep afterglow of the western sun, I am in the library of the mansion, surrounded it seemed by every art book ever printed. There is so much to choose from, I can only walk slowly along shelf after shelf with fingers sliding over binding after binding.

Miss Olhak?

I turn to see a very groomed thin, gray-haired man in an immaculate white jacket, a servant's jacket, looking at me from the doorway... looking past me actually... in fact, not looking at all. I can see from the blankness of his wide eyes that he is blind.

Yes? I answer,

He adjusts his eyes to the direction of my voice.

Mr. Pettingill asks if you would mind coming in to meet him.

Even though I'm wondering why Orlando Pettingill doesn't come in to meet me, I answer... sure.

I follow this man through a maze of corridors and he moves with the sureness of a sighted person. We come to a closed door and my guide knocks softly twice and opens the door for me.

The room is nearly dark, with slatted shutters letting in little of the last light of day. The door closes behind me and I stand in the quiet dark looking ahead at the great mass of Orlando Pettingill seated behind a desk, silhouetted against the dark wall behind him.

Frida Olhak, hello. I'm so honored you've come.

He says this in a disarmingly cultured voice.

Do you mind if we have a little light?

Yes, let's have light, I say, thrilled at the idea of really seeing his face.

But the soft desk light he turns on only illuminates me.

Oh my dear, you really are Frida, just as Hanna said.

Hanna?

Yes, she called last night and told me your whole story.

Pamé rage is streaking through me, and the most civil thing I can think to say is, Hanna is a thief and a liar, she's made it all up.

Orlando is quiet for a few seconds and finally says, I see, I have inaccurate information, I'm sorry. In any event I'm so pleased you're here.

He holds out a pale, small, hairless hand into the pool of light, and lays it over my dark and larger hand. His touch sends streaks of heat up my arm, even though his hand is damp and clammy.

Silence.

Why are you sitting in the dark, Orlando?

My directness and use of his first name cause a molecular shift in the air in the room.

Because I am grotesque to look at, Frida.

He says this with no self-pity. He could as easily have said, because I have brown eyes.

I am about to blurt out the truth, that I watched him peel off his green frog skin to thrill me with his pale, naked corpulence... But I don't, and I sit in silence for a few seconds before I ask, What about the pelicans?

Pelicans...?

Yes, your little gang of trained pelicans and your wiggly fish-eating ritual?

He is silent as he considers the possibility of my having witnessed everything up close, and therefore already knowing what he looks like.

I sensed another presence...

He then turns on a second desk lamp, this time illuminating himself.

It's as though he's suddenly surfaced from a dark pool and is sitting on a rock opposite me. He is wearing a loose silk dressing gown of rich green with a pattern of pale gray pelicans flying through it.

His dark, tight curly hair begins high on his head surrounding a large round forehead, beneath which... beneath which are enormous brown, bulging, soft, moist, wise, and sad eyes encircled by pale lids that seem to hold his eyes more out of than in their sockets. His lips are thick and wide, connecting one generous jowl to the other. He seems to have no neck and his fleshy face rests on his silky green shoulders.

I realize my next thought is actually audible when he repeats my softly spoken word.

Diego?

Diego, I repeat, allowing a space for him to consider Frida Kahlo's personal history, which I'm sure he knows if he collects her paintings.

He understands, stares intently, and says no more, but the mood in the room has softened.

What is this pelican business, Orlando?

He hesitates, watching me carefully before replying.

Tell me who you are Frida, and then I'll tell you about the pelicans.

Silence.

It'll be an equal trade of personal information.

He says this firmly as though cutting a business deal.

I am Frida Kahlo's granddaughter.

Thank you.

He smiles and swallows, as though ingesting this information and his jowls go in and out.

He is such a lovely frog prince, I giggle. Yes? He asks of my giggle.

Nothing. Now tell me about the pelicans.

He looks up as though the story is in the sky the birds inhabit, and the whites of his eyes bulge with inner images. He swallows again and his jowls inflate and deflate, and my heart flutters like the fourteen-year-old Frida.

He lowers his bulbous eyes to study me steadily like I'm a dark tadpole he is considering for a meal, but I know he's really considering how trustworthy I am to be told his secret.. But he has my secret and he knows that we made a deal, and he starts his story.

I've made large fortunes several times, and that is boring. I've collected extraordinary art (including your grandmother's paintings) and that is very unboring. But the most interesting thing I've ever done has been here at the river, here in the river.

Eleven years ago, I was sitting at the bank of the river below, squatting frog-like as I did as a child in spite of the derision that always provoked from other children... to be precise, I was known as Froggy my whole childhood.

But I knew from the beginning that I would transcend my appearance, and I did. It was easy. I was a mathematical prodigy from the age of two. and that plus an acute sense of premonition in the markets of the world, equaled profit and then wealth.

I'm not repulsed by my appearance, but I knew that others were, so all my financial dealings were done by intermediaries. And while others saw me briefly now and then, I didn't like being scrutinized, which is why I have a blind butler.

So, I was squatting below at the edge of the river and a great flock of pelicans circled several times. They were after the millions of anchovies that inhabit the river mouth periodically. But I'd never seen so many pelicans at one time before. They seemed to be led by a larger, older bird who would sweep over the water, eye a school of anchovies, and plunge in followed by the others.

After a half-hour of gorging, this pelican prince (as I came to call him) swims up past me and down past me, each time getting closer, and all the time watching me without turning his head, and finally came within two feet of me.

While the others had gray bodies and white heads, he was all white. What he thought as he studied me, of course I'll never know, but one of my speculations was that he, as the largest pelican... the pelican prince so to speak, viewed me as some frog prince, because I was so large, and looking at my face, he could clearly see I was Frog.

At this, Orlando hesitates and studies me for some clue to how I'm taking it all. He clearly wants no pity.

Yes!!! I say sitting up straight and smiling. A frog prince!!!

Orlando's smile is so broad I can easily imagine a hundred minnows swimming into his mouth at once. Now he is relaxed and he tells his story slowly and with trust.

That day, the pelican prince and I only looked carefully into each other's eyes, but I saw so much wisdom and mystery in his, I felt like what he saw in my own eyes was only a trite life.

When the prince pelican decided to take his followers out to sea, I thought I would never see him again. They rose, and circled to gain altitude as they always do, but on their last pass, he dropped down below the others and flew directly overhead, with his neck tucked in so he could look down at me.

Three days later they were all again in the river lost in a frenzy of feeding. At one point, one bird taller than the others looked over at me. This time, I sat in a foot of water in my proudest frog stance, knees bent under me, my arms straight down, and my fat jowls expanding and contracting rhythmically. I sat perfectly still and the prince swam in a circuitous route until he was just a foot away. His small wise eyes, unnervingly close together, watched me carefully but without fear. Abruptly he opened his cavernous bill, and inside his pouch were forty or fifty flashing anchovies. He held it open and studied me as though waiting for some action from me. When a few fish leapt out, he closed his bill and looked like he was losing patience. He opened it again and then I knew he was making an offering.

Without hesitation I reached into his bill, grabbed five anchovies, and wiggling in my hand, dropped them into my mouth and executed a loud froggy swallow.

The prince spread his wings out as though to applaud, but instead pointed his bill skyward to swallow the remaining maze of fish. He then flapped his wings into the water and I flapped my hands and feet into the water, and he flew off with a loud unmelodic squawk.

The prince and I did this several times that year before the pelicans flew south for the winter. The next year he returned and before he left, he had recruited six more pelicans into our ritual. And so it went year after year.

In time I acquired my wetsuit so I could seine for anchovies and participate in the exchange. The number of pelicans in our ritual grew to ten or twelve. Three years ago, the prince didn't return and I knew he had died of old age. However, one of the older pelicans assumed the role of leader and still is.

But you see, the significance of it all is that without the prince in the first place, none of it would have happened, and it is he I think of every year. And of course, if I looked any different none of it would have happened either.

Silence.

Orlando looks at me to see if I think he's a little peculiar, which of course he is. I wonder what his high-rolling business partners would think, watching him and the wriggling fish with his pelican friends... or the art dealers he buys his art from.

I am in love.

***

The next morning, I am on the terrace watching the Pacific roll into the mouth of the river, lost in thoughts of frog prince Pettingill.

From behind me I hear soft breathy sounds of music... a flute it seems... like an Andean flute. I realize Hans is playing and I stand still facing the water. (Hanna said Hans had lived for several years with a flute virtuoso.)

The music stops and I hear Hans's uneven walk as she comes alongside me and proceeds to circle me slowly, saying nothing, but eyeing me carefully. The usual small string of drool descends from her lower lip, which she ignores. She is wearing a billowy white dress that comes to her ankles.

She walks completely around me silently. During her second time around, she is staring at my eyebrows, her eyes wider than ever, and she begins to nod slightly in unison with the dip in her limp. Now she is smiling slyly and still eyeing my eyebrows as she brings her flute to her lips.

When she begins to play, I'm startled by the clarity and confidence of the sound. The notes go up and down in a counterpoint to the dip of her limp. Finally, she stops in front of me and her music is a description of the winged configuration of my eyebrows. This is emphasized by the dipping and uplifting of her legs and body as she plays. At one point her drool becomes mixed into the sound and she immediately makes it part of her music.

I briefly have the sensation I could ascend just with the power of my eyebrows, literally leave the ground. It's unnerving.

Finally, at the climax of her song, she closes her eyes and shivers as she sends sounds over the promontory, resounding out to sea. When she finishes she opens her eyes wide again to look into mine. Her eyes are filled with tears, but they are tears of creative joy, I'm certain. Then she smiles fully, her teeth white and perfect but glistening with saliva, as is her mouth.

Fri... da!

Her voice is a melodic little explosion and sends a spray of spittle in my direction, which she laughs at as she wipes her mouth with a perfect forearm.

I go down on one knee and say, Hans... where did you learn to play so beautifully?

She comes very close and stares into my eyes as though I'm to see the answer to my question there. Finally, she shrugs and turns to look out to sea.

I realize that Hans's lack of words is no frustration to her, it's other people's burden. What she has to say she says with her flute.

I leave beautiful little Hans, leaning to one side on her lame leg, flute in hand, staring out at the rolling swells of the Pacific. She seems deep in thought and I wonder, what are her thoughts? Are they complex combinations of images, of people and places and things? Are they constantly being translated into sounds that she then speaks with her flute?

I decide that if she will let me, I will paint her, and as I always learn more about myself in each self-portrait, I will learn something of Hans.

My first painting here at the mansion, though, will be one more Kahlo self-portrait. I will establish my presence here in all my Pamé power, complete with bird bones, blue teeth, and the yellow body stripes the Pamé women of centuries ago wore.

Hans's music has inspired me and I walk quickly to the large white studio Orlando (through his blind butler, Klaus) has offered me.

The next morning I prepare myself for my Pelican Reach self-portrait. My bones are in and held taut by my stretched nipples. I have painted the wide yellow stripes around myself from my ankles to my neck. I am about to apply my blue tooth dye when there is a polite knock on my studio door. I open it a crack to find Klaus standing stiffly starched in his white jacket, holding a small envelope. Klaus as usual is looking slightly past me. I am not modest about my body though no gringo has ever seen me in my full Pamé glory, but I realize that this gringo is not going to see anything anyway. I open the door.

Come in, Klaus.

He enters cautiously, sensing something different.

I have a message from Mr. Pettingill.

After he speaks he dilates his nostrils just slightly, and I realize that Klaus, like all people with one sense missing, makes up for it with another.

I have been perspiring slightly in the excitement and anticipation of my new painting and being naked, my scent has surrounded Klaus's starched presence.

He holds the envelope out toward me and there is the slightest tremor in his hand.

I wait before taking it because... because it is oddly arousing to be naked before this man, and all the more so because he can't see me.

I take the envelope and say, wait before you go, Klaus.

He stands stark still with his eyes wide but there's no clue there to what he's thinking.

My impulse is to ask Klaus to feel my sacred hawk bones. Actually, it's not my impulse, it's Grandmother Kahlo's plan; I feel her provocative presence that strongly.

The image of Klaus's fingers politely traversing the bones and of course the textured flesh gripping them triples my excitement and the next scent released in our little tent of fragrances results in a frenzy of nostril flutters.

In the end I don't do what my dear, previous Frida would have done.

I open the envelope to read Orlando's words.

I would be pleased if you would have dinner with me tonight... at eight? We will look at the Kahlo self-portraits. Klaus will come by to bring you here.

I turn to Klaus. His sightless eyes have shifted down as though to see the source of the now-dominating scent in the room. I wonder if he has ever had sight.

Tell Orlando yes, Klaus, and thank you. He turns to leave.

And Klaus...

Yes?

Have you always been blind? . He smiles for the first time.

No.

***

He was so cruel to her...

This is my first comment about the Kahlo painting we're standing in front of. It is a self-portrait, but it also includes Diego Rivera, who is standing to Frida's left. Orlando is standing to my right and it's as though we're in front of a mirror. Frida and I really are identical and she must be just my age in this painting. Orlando is much more frog-like than Diego, uglier most people would say, and he doesn't have the intensity of the artist in his face, nor the cruelty. But the huge mass of the man combined with his supreme self-assurance and wise timeless eyes gives him a regal presence in the room.

He is in another copious silk dressing gown, the color of the deep ocean, a blue close to black, a blue I long to plunge into.

On the left side of the double portrait there is a single self-portrait... Frida with a raw bloody incision down the center of her upper body and encircled by crude white straps as though holding her intact, a reference to one of the brutal operations after her accident.

On the right side is Frida with close cropped hair, dressed in a man's suit with a black monkey on her shoulder. In both paintings she is severe, angry, and unhappy.

She suffered so... Orlando says this softly as he pours us each another deep green liqueur, which even though it's slightly sweet, has a mysterious quality of ocean depths to its flavor.

Our whole evening has seemed under water. We are in a small gallery with dark green-blue walls on which there are only the three Kahlo paintings. Before Orlando turned on the horizontal gallery lamps over each painting, the room was almost dark. What light there was came through the slatted shutters... reflections from the salt-water pool outside lighted from beneath. This gives the room the quality of a cube of ocean, lanced by dim sunlight slanting through seaweed.

We ate dinner here earlier, served flawlessly by Klaus, whose nostrils flared slightly when he leaned over my shoulder to serve me.

All evening Orlando has looked from Kahlo painting to me to Kahlo painting and I have looked at him looking. He is wary though, still suspicious of my desire to observe him so carefully, but since he has his own desire to observe my Frida Kahlo face, we have made our unspoken deal. We look at each other silently a lot.

At one point he said, you are such an exact replica of Frida Kahlo, and I said with annoyance... I am Frida Kahlo!

And when I said this, we both knew I meant it in both senses, something that only since being here, have I felt so strongly.

When I leave his dark aquatic realm that night, I say... Tomorrow, I'll show you my Frida.

I mean the diary and he knows it and his great fleshy mouth expands to a smile of child-like delight.

***

You know, of the two, Frida was by far the better painter...

Orlando and I are sitting side by side on a settee in yet another gallery room, a room with light green walls, like sunlit shallow waters.

He is dismissing Diego Rivera's importance in art in a way that seems protective of Kahlo, and I sense that aside from his connoisseur's interest in her painting, Orlando has had a long romance with Frida Kahlo in the vivid realm of his imagination.

It has always troubled me that your grandmother was so obsessed by, one could say, addicted to Rivera. He treated her so dreadfully. I've always wondered where that came from, but this gives some clues doesn't it?

We have the diary between us and Orlando is pointing to Frida's drawing of the great round Pamé, his face frog-like, lying impassively on his back while the young Frida, the skirt of her school uniform hiked up, is straddling him. Her small thighs are barely able to circle his girth. She seems to be initiating everything, and seems possessed by the whole business, smiling slyly, her eyebrows darkly declaring her determination.

I shift on the settee so that my own small Frida thigh rests against Orlando's, full and fleshy.

I say, well maybe she saw it all as a challenge. In both cases she was much younger, and both the Pamé and Diego had great power and she had none. With the Pamé she was just a school girl, literally, and he was a chief, and with Diego, Frida was a novice painter and he was already famous. And the bigness of the two men?... maybe there was an Everest element to it. You know, the challenge of conquering the mountain... getting to the top and straddling the surface... feeling the thrill of the adventure penetrate her.

Oh my, Orlando exclaims as he looks down at the floor where the diary has just crashed after slipping from his fingers. He sits immobile, staring down at the diary, his great jowls expanding and contracting as though he's about to shoot out a long reptilian tongue to snatch up the book, and the Frida in it.

Finally, he says, I'm sorry, that was clumsy of me. He hands me the diary as though no longer qualified to hold it.

I take the book and cup my dark Kahlo hand over his, gringo-pale and clammy.

You're forgiven, Orlando.

I have become infatuated with his name, so full of round sounds, like the form of the frog prince himself.

My days have flowed into weeks and into a routine, and my painting has flourished. Each day I stand before my full-length mirror, my naked body striped with yellow, my nipples pierced with bone, my teeth blue with Pamé power.

My portrait is nearly finished and each morning, as I prepare myself for the character I play in the painting (the real Pamé player is in the painting), I feel like an actor coming closer and closer to closing night. And with each performance I find myself more and more frenzied, taken back into a ritual a century or two in the past.

***

It is the pounding drumbeat that inspires my most savage blue-toothed grimace, as I let out my short primal shrieks and, paint brush in hand, stare at myself in the mirror.

Then the drumming has suddenly ceased, and reflected in the mirror I see a mammoth Pamé frog chief. In one leap, I am completely turned around, legs apart, my mouth open wide to bare my blue power-teeth, my nipple bones vibrating rapidly from the motion, and my yellow stripes quaking from my rapid panting.

Ohhhh... I heard your shrieks and... I've been knocking and when you didn't answer I...

But Orlando doesn't finish because he has slumped to the floor of my studio.

I approach him cautiously. He is on his back, his large limbs awry, his lovely frog face pale and green. His great girth projects upward, and it is there I will join him.

Gripping silky black fabric, I pull myself upward, finally sliding one small striped Frida thigh high up, over and around, triumphantly straddling my frog prince. As I am about to slide my hands inside Orlando's satin dressing gown, Klaus 's voice slips politely into the room.

Excuse me, I've been knocking...

He stands staring slightly over my head. Orlando has revived and his bulbous eyes are rolled upward, looking back over his forehead toward Klaus's voice.

Klaus continues, You have a visitor...

Into the doorway steps Hanna, with a bemused and malevolent smile. Behind her is little Hans, as wide-eyed as Klaus. My Pamé power has brought about its usual spectacle. Here I am striped, pierced, and blue-toothed, still straddling poor Orlando, who has closed his aquatic eyes rather than witness any more of this theater of the absurd.

***

So, eyebrows, are you and the frog fucking?

Hanna and I are alone in my studio. Orlando has made his exit with surprising dignity, Klaus and Hans trailing behind, hand-in-hand, the lame leading the blind.

But this is not the Hanna I last saw in San Francisco. She has shaved her head and has three gold loops in her left nostril. She is wearing a sheer, pale lavender shift that comes to just above her bare feet, one of which has had its round red scar transformed by a tattoo into the angry pupil of a glaring eye. Her dress is near-transparent and her firm breasts and buttocks repeatedly beat at the fabric as she moves about.

Whether the frog and I are fucking, Hanna, is none of your fucking business.

This bit of acerbity, matching hers, neutralizes the mood of the room.

Hanna says quietly, you' re right Frida.

And then she adds in her surprising way of reversing everything... You are so strangely beautiful in your stripes, and your bones (sorry I borrowed them for a few days), and your cobalt teeth.

She is silent for a few moments, looking down at her hand scars, and then continues carefully.

You see Frida, I hate you because you're the only person I've met who is as strong as I am.

Silence.

But I also love you for the same reason. Silence.

I have something to ask of you Frida. Yes?

Hanna now stares at my near-finished full length Pamé self-portrait.

Will you puncture my nipples for my bones, and then paint my portrait?

I am about to say no to piercing her, until she mentions my painting her portrait, and the image of her standing, head shaved, nipples bone-pierced, and with her red stigmata scars flaunted as she always does, is too intriguing a subject to refuse. Besides, painting her will give me power over her, in the most primal cave-painter's sense.

***

Will it hurt, Frida?

Yes, it hurts, the pain is part of the ritual. I was twelve when this was done to me, and I didn't utter a sound.

Are you ready for my assistance?

Klaus is at the door of my studio, staring in sightlessly at the scene in front of him. We need Klaus's assistance because Hanna's hands must be held down. Klaus does not know what is going to take place tonight, but he agreed to help when Orlando asked him if he would, no questions asked.

Hanna is on her back on the floor, nude. I am straddling her, painted in my yellow stripes, bones in place, teeth blue and bared.

In my hand I have the very tool used to pierce my nipples ten years ago. It is a hollow round bird bone about an eighth of an inch in diameter. Its tip is razor sharp. A piece of flesh the size of the interior of the bone is excised in this ritual, thus allowing the insertion of the tapered bird bones, which Hanna will then wear.

Klaus takes his place on the floor, kneeling, his hands firmly gripping Hanna's wrists, which are stretched above her head, flat on the floor.

Hanna's nipples are frightened and congealed, but she has asked for this and I have no sympathy... on the contrary, this is a gift from me.

Ready Hanna...?

Yes.

I stretch her left nipple up between my thumb and forefinger, pulling her breast into a cone shape. The piercing bone easily slices into her as I rotate it rapidly back and forth.

My weight can barely pin down Hanna's hips as she writhes side to side, her back arched skyward. Klaus is using all his strength to hold her wrists in place, his face like the facade of a movie theater where inside a bizarre film is playing.

When the piercing bone comes out the other side of Hanna's nipple, I gently retrieve it, and Hanna collapses to the floor. She has not made a sound, but tears have flooded her eyes. She sobs softly (my guess is that Hanna rarely cries) while I wait for her word to do the other side.

Okay, Frida, do the other one.

I do, and when I'm finished, I ask Klaus to release Hanna's hands, and when he does she immediately cups them protectively over her breasts and cries quietly.

For his part, Klaus's nostrils have been doing the jitterbug in response to the copious perspiration of Hanna and me and the secretion of who knows what other scents.

He stands then, and when I say thank you Klaus, he says you're most welcome and leaves the room with the same formality as if he's just served tea.

Hanna is still shaken when she leaves, but humbly (for Hanna) thanks me and kisses me on the mouth.

She will spend a couple of weeks caring for herself, keeping the openings open and guarding against infection. I have told her what she needs to do. I don't expect to see Hanna for a while... the ritual is a very introspective one.

***

From where I stand, he could be bottom-feeding. Orlando is frog-kicking deep in his heated salt-water pool. He is nude. I didn't expect him here. He has kept a distance since he fainted on my studio floor, collapsed at the sight of me at my savage best. I certainly didn't intend that he lose his balance and his bearings (as I did with my gringo lover at his wedding).

When Orlando comes back up the length of the pool he is on his back, still under water but closer to the surface. I know he can't see me as I can see him, the green pool is softly lit, but I am surrounded by darkness. As he passes below me I see that he is erect, very erect, like a World War II U-boat patrolling for enemy ships.

I laugh. He is such a boy frog.

***

It's El Nino that has confused them.

Orlando is explaining why the pelicans are breeding this far north for the first time ever. We are in his gray-green custom-made kayak paddling up the river to where yesterday he discovered the courting pelicans.

The warm water and air temperatures have confused them, and excited them.

There is a breathless quality to Orlando's voice as he softly talks.

It is just dawn and the river is a mirror. The sky is a soft rose and the sun is just streaking over the hills to the east onto the hills to the west. My eyes are filled with tears at such beauty, and with the memory of last night's aquatic adventure that began because I couldn't resist slipping into the pool with my frog prince.

I clung to Orlando and in his excitement, he propelled us wildly in circles through the warm salt water... propelled us with powerful frog kicks, each time thrusting up into me with the force to lift us both out of the water. At his final thrust he filled me with so much fluid that as we calmly continued to circle the pool I left a creamy streak from between my own frog-thrusting legs strung behind us like loopy aquatic jet trails.

As I sit behind Orlando this morning, lovingly holding his great waist as he gently propels us upriver with the dipping strokes of his paddle, more of his fluid gift is trickling down my thigh from his thrusts into me an hour ago, just before we left his bed.

Orlando now holds his paddle still as we glide along the marsh grasses of the island we're circling.

Oh... I can't help saying softly.

In an area of matted grass, forty or fifty pelicans are promenading in pairs. Their angular wings are out, spanning six or seven feet, and moving in spastic patterns as the birds do their forty-million-year-old love waltz. Stepping carefully on their big webbed feet they circle each other, flaunting their golden head feathers and staring with pale blue eyes circled with bright pink skin.

Orlando explains that all this coloring appears only during breeding... he's never seen it before.

Our kayak bumps into a half-submerged log, and the closest pelican looks over as though we're a pair of peeping toms. Orlando backs us out of view, turns the kayak around, and paddles us to a grassy slope at the opposite bank of the river. He puts one foot in the water, takes my hand and pulls me impatiently through mud and down into moist grasses.

Our clothes are off in seconds and Orlando is up inside of me stretching and reaching spasmodically. He is irrational with arousal and the fact that we're now half in the water is irrelevant, or very relevant, and is my last rational thought. Just before Orlando spurts me to bursting. there is a cacophony of raucous squawks from the orgy at the rookery across the water.

At the moment of Orlando's spew inside of me, I have an epiphany... but I won't say what, yet.

***

Three months have passed, Hanna is healed, and I am at work on my painting of her. I spend my nights and a little bit of my days too with Orlando because Klaus suddenly left Pelican Reach without a word of explanation. One morning he was simply gone. Orlando was philosophic about it. There's an explanation for every-thing, he said over coffee the morning Klaus disappeared.

However, he reported the disappearance to the police and since Klaus was blind, they came out to do an investigation (against Orlando's wishes... he said they've wanted to go through the mansion for years). No sign of foul play was found and the investigation was closed.

***

One morning while Hanna and I are at work on the painting, after an hour of silence Hanna announces...

I'm fucking the gardener.

The gardener, Henry Stern... we fuck every day in his house by the tool shed. He is German, and I like to talk sex in my own language.

As Hanna speaks, I remember my encounter with the gardener the day I arrived... that sinister, skinny, dark-haired man with a pistol on his belt.

All I say is, Henry Stern doesn't sound very German to me.

Hanna laughs... it's probably an alias, as we Germans all have our dark secret pasts.

***

My painting of Hanna is almost finished. Between us we decided what it would be and it is strange and strong.

Hanna is painted on a cross (we made a large one from two pieces of wood pier washed up on the beach). The cross was Hanna's idea, a prop she and her brother used in a performance in Berlin.

Her bones are in place (she chose two from an osprey we found on the beach). They are Y shaped and pushed into her nipples with the V on the outside. A bird of prey, she said with satisfaction when we found it.

Her hands are up on the cross piece and her feet are one over the other on the vertical piece. Over her red scars I have painted a purple larkspur instead of spikes.

With her bald head, stigmata scars, and pierced nipples, Hanna is one-third Buddha, one-third Christ, and one-third Pagan.

This morning we are at work early in the studio. Hanna stands against the cross and I am correcting the curve of her waist and hip. Hanna is tired and irritable.

Thoughts of Klaus enter my head.

I miss Klaus.

Silence.

There was something mysterious behind his blindness.

Silence.

I continue to paint for another ten minutes. The room is quiet until Hanna makes her statement like a pistol shot.

I killed Klaus.

For a second, I think Hanna is serious, then I laugh and continue painting.

I killed Klaus.

Now Hanna is looking directly at me and her eyes are telling the truth.

He was an East German guard, at the wall, he killed my people, Henry Stern told me. I confronted Klaus and he said yes, but...

I didn't wait to hear his justification, that he was just following orders, for they all say the same thing. I locked him up and starved him. No one will ever find him and if you say anything to anyone, I'll deny I ever told you.

Hanna is still staring at me defiant as I run to Orlando, the only thing I can think of to do. He returns with me immediately to the studio where Hanna has just finished dressing.

In seconds Orlando has Hanna pinned to her chair with the intensity of his eyes that I have never seen so large.

He wastes no time...

Klaus was in the East German army and against his will was assigned to the Berlin Wall. But he could not shoot anyone. During the first shooting that took place under his watch, at the sight of a woman killed in her effort to go over the wall, he was struck blind, literally... his blindness is psychosomatic. It was documented in his GDR records, which I have seen. He was dishonorably discharged from the army, and a year later, he himself escaped over the wall, aided by his wife, who was killed in the process.

Hanna is stunned.

Take me to Klaus now, Hanna!

We follow Hanna through a labyrinth of hallways in the basement of the mansion. She leads us to a secret wine cellar that Klaus had discovered and told her about, where he would go to sip the priceless vintage reds of the previous owners of the mansion.

Once inside the wine cellar, there is a concealed and locked door, whose key Hanna quickly locates. When Orlando opens it his flashlight reveals a macabre scene.

Klaus is on his back on the floor with a rat in his mouth. We are paralyzed with shock. The only movement is, miraculously, one finger of the hand Klaus has across his chest.

***

It is now a month since we removed poor Klaus from his would-be death chamber.

It was his blindness that saved his life. Because the room was black, it was he who had the advantage over the rats. It's true they bit him without mercy, but because his hearing was so acute, he regularly managed to grab a rat as it approached for an attack. He would break its neck and, unbelievably, eat it raw. After two weeks without food it was his involuntary will to survive that enabled him to do this. And when the rats learned to noiselessly approach him, it was his highly honed sense of smell that granted him his hunting skill.

When Klaus returns from the hospital in not yet normal health (he is still thin, pale, and nervous), only he forgave Hanna, and he steadfastly refused to bring any criminal charges against her.

When I ask him for an explanation, he looks past me, his eyes narrowing slightly as he looks into history.

You see, life in the East, in the GDR, was so inhumane, so testing of one's last traces of decency that anyone could be turned into a murderer. Trust disappeared from everyday life, neighbors reported on each other to the Stasi, the secret police. People vanished never to be heard from again.

And remember what happened to Hanna and her brother on the wall.

Klaus is silent for a few moments. Then he adds ominously.

Hanna will never be the same as she was before she scaled the Wall, never.

Silence.

And neither will I.

Then I ask Klaus about Henry Stern the gardener, who told Hanna about Klaus's past.

Yes, this man Stern (not his real name I suspect) was also in the military and I have always had my suspicions about him. I have a friend in Berlin who has access to military files. I'll contact him and find out who Stern really is, or more accurately, was.

As Klaus talks, I wonder if he knows Hanna was fucking Henry Stern when he told her about Klaus.

***

A month later, Hanna and I are standing before my nearly completed painting of little Hans. She is nude in the painting, at her insistence, because I was in mine, and her mother was in hers.

She has also gone to great effort to explain to me that she wants her nipples pierced, as mine are, and her mother's are. I have agreed to do it (Hanna immediately said yes) but not until Hans turns twelve, in another month, my age when mine were pierced.

For her painting, little Hans sat unblinking, on an old embroidered bench, while we've worked together every day for several hours. She stares straight ahead. One arm is straight out supporting her weight and her smaller leg is bent and resting on the bench. Her body is pale, rounded, and perfect... emerging breasts the size of half-oranges topped with delicate pink nipples, which I cringe at the thought of piercing... perfect round arms, narrow waist, no hips, and a sculptured small pubis with the slightest dusting of soft hairs.

This kind of beauty fascinates me because it's so transient, changing each day to eventually disappear and become the beauty of Hans as an adult.

Hanna says softly, her German accent more clipped than usual, you know there is the presence of her father in my daughter.

I remain silent. A full minute passes. Klaus and I, we are fucking.

Hanna says this with the same detachment as when she told me three months ago that she had killed him. She continues...

A week ago I went to his room. He heard my presence, but didn't ask who it was... he could smell me. I circled his bed and watched his nostrils, which were like a barometer. No word was said. I removed my clothes and kneeled on his bed. He remained immobile, staring at the invisible ceiling. I passed body part after body part above his face. When I kneeled over him, one leg on either side of his face, still not touching him, I said, Klaus, forgive me for trying to be your murderer.

Tears filled his eyes, and he said, you come from Leipzig, don't you Hanna? I can smell it. My wife came from Leipzig, our great center of Germanic culture; Bach, Wagner, Goethe, Schiller, Mendelssohn, Nietzsche...

Finally, I lay down next to Klaus. We spent that night together, and every night since.

Hanna then looks at me with a disarming smile, laughs lightly like a sixteen-year-old, and says in her thickest German accent...

Now I luff Klaus!

This wild mood swing in one conversation makes me more wary of Hanna than ever.

Another month passes and the mansion receives one more shock.

We are all at the dinner table, including Orlando, who has finally chosen to believe me when I tell him he is not grotesque, but beautiful. We are listening to his mother, who is striving to keep together the components of a story she's telling, when we hear the faint sounds of Han's flute enter the mansion at a side door a long corridor away.

As the notes move closer, we become silent because the music is so strangely beautiful and moving. It is loud, the loudest I've ever heard Hans play, and when she finally enters the dining room, it's as loud as trumpets announcing regal presence, and appropriately so.

Behind Hans is Klaus, with eyes as alert as a forest creature, moving from face to face along the table.

Han's triumphant performance ends with a spray of spittle as she tries to put more glory into her flute than will fit.

Then she turns to Klaus, pointing to his eyes and beaming with pride.

There is total pandemonium. After everyone has somewhat settled down, Klaus tells his story. He looks carefully into one set of eyes after another as he speaks.

For three days I have been mysteriously drawn outside by the playing of this little one.

He puts his hand lovingly on the side of Hans's face, who is in turn staring at Klaus as though he is her creation.

Klaus continues.

Her music was beyond my resistance. I would stop whatever I was doing and follow her, and each day I was led farther from the mansion and more into totally unfamiliar terrain, where I would stumble and occasionally fall to the ground, but still I couldn't resist following the music.

Finally, today, just one hour ago, while being led along the headlands at the water's edge, a tricky bit of virtuosity on Hans's part led me to a point where... where she lured me forward with such promising melody, I was crying... lured me to a precipice I stepped off of and started a free fall, from which I was certain I would die, and suddenly I opened my eyes... of course my eyes were already open. What I mean is that I opened my vision, my sight! I chose to see after all these years, see once more before I died.

Klaus then bursts into tears.

Hans steps forward, a string of drool descending from her lip, and pats Klaus's head reassuringly as though to say, you really needn't have worried. I knew what I was doing all along.

Klaus continues... I did not go off the bluff of course, but fell about ten feet into a crevasse on the other side of which this one was playing to lead me on. The bottom of the crevasse was filled with soft pine boughs Hans had been putting there for a week.

Klaus hesitates a moment and then adds with total conviction...

She knew precisely what she was doing and more important, she knew she would succeed.

We all turn to look at Hans.

As she wipes the drool from her mouth, she nods her head twice in supreme self-assurance.

Klaus then scrutinizes everyone... this is the first time he's seen any of us. He can't take his eyes off Hanna.

Hanna dear, I thought I could feel all your beauty with my hands but I did not come close.

And Hanna is beautiful. She has let her hair grow... it's about an inch long and soft. She has removed her nose rings and has an expression of calm and gentleness since she and Klaus have become lovers. She looks almost sweet. I don't trust any of it.

When Klaus looks at Orlando, he can't hide his reaction to the great frog prince. But Orlando takes this graciously. He's used to it.

When Klaus turns to me, he can't take his eyes off my eyebrows (he has already apologized to all of us for his staring) and asks if he might touch them. I tell him yes but he must also go look at Grandmother Kahlo's self-portraits.

But it is little Hans that Klaus looks at most carefully. We all know now that she has profound and frightening powers, and Klaus has experienced them firsthand.

He speaks to us all as he looks at Hans.

This little one has totally taken over my will with her music, she could have done anything with me.

For a split second a brief reflection of fear passes over Hans's face... fear at her own power.

***

It is now winter, which here in Northern California means rain and high winds. On a particularly wild night, we are sitting by one of the massive fireplaces in the mansion, this one in a room filled with Orlando's collection of early Gothic painting and sculpture, images laden with apocalyptic tales. Klaus has his own tale, as medieval as any in the room. He is sitting with his left side to the fire, which casts his right side in ominous shadow, as he delivers his stunning news. In his hand is a letter he's received today from Germany.

His face clouds as he speaks...

I have long had my suspicions about Henry Stern, the gardener, so some weeks past I searched his quarters while he was in town. I found papers with his real name on them... Heinrich Stoller... and I wrote to a man in Berlin who has access to military records, to learn about this Stoller.

This was in a letter I received today...

***

My dear friend Klaus,

It gave me great pleasure to be of assistance to you in finding the following information about this Heinrich Stoller, whom you wrote to me about.

Stoller was a corporal in the army here and assigned to patrol duty at the Wall. Before that his records show nothing of note, but after arriving at the Wall, it repulses me to say, he was decorated twice for fervent marksmanship in murdering our compatriots.

On two occasions, 3 May 1985 and 11 July 1985, he was commended for halting escapes. On 3 May, he shot and killed a fifty-three-year-old man. On 11

July, he shot and killed four nineteen and twenty-year-old students, and wounded two others who managed to escape. He was...

But Klaus is interrupted by a wine glass pitched into the fireplace with such force it pulverizes.

Hanna is standing and shaking uncontrollably.

Immediately, we all realize who those two students were that escaped the gardener's bullets, wounded and leaving behind their four dead friends.

Klaus embraces Hanna to steady her as she savagely grows, I'll kill him, I'll kill the fucker, I'll kill him.

***

An hour later we are discussing strategy. Orlando is trying to convince Hanna that she cannot take justice into her own hands, that to kill the gardener would mean prison for her.

Hanna insisted. To send him back to Germany for trial would only end in one more drawn-out discussion of who was responsible, the order-giver or the order-follower.

Even after Hanna admits she would go to jail if she killed Heinrich Stoller, probably for a long time, the last thing she says is...

If I don't kill him, nobody will.

We have decided to give no clues to Stoller until the German authorities are notified, and he can be extradited to Germany. He could easily disappear to live elsewhere under one more alias.

Orlando turns the whole matter over to one of his lawyers. We try to return to our routines, although each of us is concerned that Hanna, finally, will be unable to control her rage.

***

Then one evening we hear the intriguing sound of Hans's flute out some distance from the mansion. Klaus notices the gardener listening carefully and then walking in the direction of the music. He returns in an hour.

The next night the same thing happens, only a little later, and I realize what Hans has in mind. I think all of us know, but we don't talk about it. We are silent accomplices.

On the third night, the gardener doesn't return. On the fourth night it is silent.

The next day Klaus takes Hanna and me to the crevasse Hans had led him to. At the bottom is the body of Heinrich Stoller, contorted terribly. The velocity of his fall had driven him into a jagged wedge from which all the soft pine boughs had been removed, making his fall over twenty feet.

One of the gardener's eyes is visible, staring up in puzzlement as though to ask how this came about.

No word is spoken. Hanna is impassive as she looks down at the man who killed her friends, filled her and her brother with terrible bullet wounds, and only a month ago filled her with his fascist phallus.

On the walk back to the mansion, Hanna says...

As I stood there looking down at his body, I imagined the times he looked down on his silent victims. An eye for an eye.

Then after a moment she adds...

He's the one I should have locked in the wine cellar with the rats and no food.

Then she holds tight to Klaus and cries quietly.

***

Orlando tells his lawyer to cease contact with the German authorities, and after three days, calls the state police to report the gardener's absence...

He would occasionally go into town to drink, he said, and not return for a couple of days.

The gardener had gone to great lengths to live anonymously in this country. He left no family, no friends, and no history (other than with us). Klaus had already removed any of the gardener's papers with the name Heinrich Stoller on them.

It could be years, perhaps decades, before the gardener's remains are discovered. The ravens, rats, and gulls have already begun their feasting. It's a fine twist that the rats that saved Klaus's life are gorging on Heinrich Stoller's lifelessness.

***

None of us ever again discusses what we saw in the crevasse.

For her part, Hans seems only slightly affected by what she did. I occasionally catch her frowning slightly in introspection as she limps through the mansion, contemplating her powers... she has, after all, given sight and taken a life, all before the age of twelve.

***

On her birthday, Hans reminds me, with precise mime, that I promised to pierce her nipples. Now, knowing she has powers to rival any Pamé, the ritual seems not only permissible, but appropriate.

On the night of Hans's piercing, when she comes to me naked, I paint her in yellow stripes, and dye her teeth blue... all before a mirror so she can watch. I have already asked her if she wants to be a Pamé and she immediately nods. Tonight, she beams with pride and wonder at what we're doing. I have assumed the right to grant Pamé status to Hans, and if my ancestors disagree, let them strike me dead. Klaus is in the room tonight. Hans insisted. We don't know why, but my guess is that the power we're acknowledging in her with this ritual is the power that restored Klaus 's vision, and what could make more sense than having Klaus be witness with the vision Hans has granted him.

One more complex thought worked out in Hans's mind without the benefit of words.

***

Hanna is holding Han's hands down, and as she does, looking into Han's eyes, I sense what a complicated relationship there is between this mother and daughter.

I take my place, straddling Hans, permitting no more of my weight to press down on her than will be necessary to hold her in place.

Klaus is standing in a far corner, a reluctant witness.

I was just twelve when this was done to me, Hans... She nods.

Are you ready?

Hans nods.

I pull up her soft delicate right nipple and easily penetrate it. I know the pain is severe because Hans's eyes have quickly widened. But otherwise she has not moved, there are not even tears in her eyes. It's then I realize that the will that led two grown men to follow her music unquestioningly, each to his different destiny, is the same will that tonight has commanded her threshold for pain.

When I've done her other nipple, she releases a great breath of air, sits up, and admires her new perforations, into which will go the bones we've chosen together... delicate wing bones of a baby snowy egret we found on the bank of the river.

With her chin still down on her chest, Hans raises her eyes, then eyebrows, and gives me a smile that proves I've done the right thing.

During all of this, Klaus has remained still as a statue, but from his expression I can see how moved he is.

When Hans limps from the room, still in her yellow stripes, she is looking down at her small round breasts. I know she is imagining her bones in place, but what kind of new power is she imagining those bones granting her?

Three

It's so frightening, my dear.

This is Orlando's comment as we look at my just finished portrait. In this painting, Orlando is on the left, larger than life in his silky dark blue dressing gown.

I am on the right, in a long pale red Mexican-style dress.

In between us, one of her hands held by each of us, is a very small child, ageless in expression as she intently scrutinizes the world before her... scrutinizes with penetrating dark eyes beneath her one-winged Frida Kahlo eyebrow.

It's so frightening, Orlando repeats. What if she looks like me?

I have made this painting because, like the Frida before me, who told her friends at the Preparatoria that her life ambition was to have a baby with Diego Rivera, I also want a baby with my frog prince.

This painting is a talisman, to assure me my baby will be a Frida. I have been filled with a Kahlo fecundity for weeks, during the whole process of this painting.

I am asking Orlando for his baby. I don't want to just surprise him (as my grandmother is nudging me to do). Mine is a plan. I know my fertility cycle well.

All right, Frida, but if she has little webbed feet... well, you had fair warning.

Funny as this sounds, it's not a joke. One morning, in an extensive and compulsive inventory I took of Orlando's many fascinating anatomical details, I discovered that he does in fact have webbed feet. It's not obvious, but if one is, say, to stretch Orlando's toes apart in order to, say, use one in an impulsively lascivious manner, then the webbing is there to be seen, and is a lovely pale translucent green.

***

Pelican Reach itself is teeming with promise of fertility, even aside from my own plan for the ultimate self-portrait.

Hans, one month after her piercing, limps into my studio wrapped in a large white bath towel. Her eyes are bright with excitement as she drops the towel to the floor in a grand gesture of presentation.

Her snowy egret bones are in place, and her little breasts are carefully circled with red. Blood red, in fact, actual blood, I realize as I also see a red streak down the inside of her lame thigh. Hans sits down on a chair opposite me, pulling her legs up and apart and pointing first to her nipples and then to her small cleft and its ribbon of red drool.

She is convinced that her first period is really the result of her piercing, and to her it is one more magical dimension of the ritual.

When Hanna and I each in our own turn show her the blood between our legs, to let her know that it happens to all women, Hans quickly points to our pierced nipples to prove her point.

We consider enlisting one of the maids to show Hans both her menstrual blood and her unpierced nipples, but in the end, we decide Hans's chosen beliefs have more value than factual knowledge.

***

The third Pelican Reach event in the fertility field comes when Hanna announces to me that she is pregnant.

The problem is that she had conceived the baby in the transition period when she went from the gardener as sex partner to Klaus as lover, and she doesn't know who the father is.

She says in her objective Germanic manner.

The father is either Stoller, the Satan, or Klaus, the saint.

It is a dilemma. I am glad is not mine. That is the smug thought I have... before I find out differently.

***

One morning over coffee, Orlando gives me curious news. Frida, you remember in my letters to you, back in the beginning, when I said I knew about the existence of the diary, and about the death of your mother, and was told about the quality of your paintings...? Well, all that information came from one person, who I'm happy to say is coming for a visit.

But who is it?

This is a man who I met quite by chance four years ago at an auction. There was a Frida Kahlo being auctioned... it was almost exactly like the one I own of Frida in a man's suit with the monkey on her shoulder. I didn't make a bid. However, this man was successful in his bid for the painting.

After the bidding, he and I talked about art, and Frida Kahlo in particular. He was young, very wealthy, very sensitive, and knowledgeable as a collector.

While we were talking about your grandmother's painting, he told me about your paintings, and subsequently, about the diary and your mother. He told me too that you were Frida's granddaughter. But he was very evasive about the source of all this information and I didn't know what to believe and what not to believe.

He did however give me the address where I wrote to you, and he gave me the reverse spelling of your name, which you were using.

What is his name, Orlando? Peter Cunningham.

But I don't know any Peter Cunningham, Orlando.

I ask him for a description, and I get only a vague picture... tall, fair, tasteful dresser, handsome, perhaps too much so, etc.

***

When I walk into the library that evening, to meet the mystery man, every remote possibility that went through my mind during the day pales by comparison to the reality.

Standing before me is my gringo lover of four years ago. No, I killed my gringo lover of four years ago. Standing before me is a clone of my gringo lover, a twin of my gringo lover, and it is the word twin that stirs a vague recollection.

My lover, whose name was Paul, Paul Lattimore, once made a brief reference to an estranged brother in explaining a complicated family rupture that had occurred early in his life.

His mother and father divorced, and because there was huge wealth, but only on one side (I don't remember which). the fortune was not only divided with great hostility all around, but the family too. One brother remained with the father, using his name, and one with the mother, using her name.

But Paul never told me his brother was an identical twin, a fact embodied by the man standing before me.

All of this has raced through my mind in seconds as I observe this man observing me.

And what has raced through my heart is troubling.

When I first met Paul, five years ago, my physical attraction to him was instant. fervent. and infectious... as in fatal infection.

Of course, the fatal part was the other way around and this reassurance allows me to take this man's hand when he is introduced to me, but what I don't know now is that he will take not only my hand, but all of me, to the great detriment of all of us.

You're Paul's brother.

I say this immediately after Orlando has introduced us.

I guess it's pretty obvious, isn't it, he says in a manner disarmingly like Paul's.

And obvious it is. He has the same lean, graceful height, fine hands (one of which holds onto mine too long), thick blond hair, fair skin, high intelligent forehead, aristocratic nose, soft eyes too blue, full mouth too full of provocative playfulness as he speaks, revealing his fine perfect white rich boy's teeth. His perfect white teeth are welcome to perfectly imbed themselves playfully in any private part of my anatomy for as long as his fucking beautiful self would like to. Please grand-mother, invoke the frog prince power to protect me from everything here that dear loving Orlando isn't.

***

Dinner is devoted mostly to discussion of the art collections of Peter and Orlando. Peter has three Kahlo paintings and surprises me by saying that he also owns three of mine, bought anonymously (I thought at the time, having not been at the gallery for my show of paintings in San Francisco two years ago).

Orlando, after much discussion of my grandmother and her paintings, says with eerie innocence... it seems Peter and I have both had a life-long romance with Frida Kahlo.

All the mansion regulars are at dinner. Orlando's mother (who in an unnerving lapse, asks how long Peter and I have been together)... Klaus (who now eats at the table, but insists on continuing as Orlando's butler)... Hanna (who watches Peter Cunningham very carefully and with too much interest)... and Hans (who watches Peter Cunningham very carefully and very skeptically).

***

When you first started seeing my brother, Frida, I saw the two of you on the streets of the city a few times.

Peter Cunningham and I are walking on the beach below the mansion.

My brother and I would occasionally cross paths back then, and once, when I saw him, I suggested a reconciliation between us. After all, it was our parent's doing that caused our breach. He agreed, and we spent some time together. It was then we talked about you and he told me about your life, your grandmother, the diary, etc. I wanted to meet you. I was fascinated with you, but Paul refused, said his life, his relationships, were none of my business.

Actually, he was wary of me because he knew you were drawn to his looks. Excuse me for sounding immodest, but we were both always aware of the effect our physical appearance has on women, and he and I were so identical.

But we did continue to see each other occasionally, so in time I also knew that he was seeing Susan, the woman he had kept a secret from you (as he kept you a secret from her, right up to the time he married her).

My brother was not a good man, he didn't deserve you, and even though I was saddened by his death, I felt it was justified retribution on the part of God. His heart attack, his death, was God's will.

My will...

Excuse me?

Paul's death was my will... I killed him. Didn't he tell you about my Pamé heritage, my Pamé power?

He laughs. Well, just because your nipples are...

He catches himself and there is alarm in his eyes. Just because my nipples are what?

Look, I'm sorry... I don't like talking about my brother's death.

My nipples are what?

I am now glaring fiercely, and I can feel his mind racing to regain some of his suave equilibrium.

Well... pierced.

And how do you know this, gringo?

Look, I'm sorry Frida, that was crude of me. I meant it lightly as part of your joking about killing him. I know you were crushed by his betrayal of you. I really don't remember where I got that information... perhaps he mentioned it to me... perhaps I read about the tradition of Pamé women. I've done a lot of research there, because...

I know his brother didn't tell him because he was too jealous and guarded and possessive.

And I know he didn't read it anywhere, because the sacred traditions of the Pamé women have been an oral history only.

He is unnerved and continues to apologize and ask my forgiveness, and looks at me sadly with his much-too-blue eyes and smiles shyly with his too-sculpted mouth revealing his too-perfect lightly flesh-biting teeth.

Finally, I give him a small laugh and say...

What have you been doing, you gringo pervert, looking through my keyhole?

He is hugely relieved at my willingness to let the whole thing go and asks me graciously if I'll drive up the coast with him tonight for dinner at the small exclusive French restaurant, which I've heard about, but never been to.

I shrug and say sure, but you won't get in there without a reservation.

I have a reservation.

This bit of self-assurance, so like his late brother, is one more annoyance, so when we get back to the mansion, I say in parting...

And, gringo? (This, I've decided will be his name.) Yes?

I killed your brother. Don't make light of what you can't comprehend.

A small black cloud glides over his much-too-blue eyes.

***

At dusk we drive up the coast in his silver BMW. Everything about him is light and luminous... like his brother, who was drawn to me because I was his absolute opposite.

When we enter the restaurant, everyone looks over to observe our absolute oppositeness. He is ten years older, ten inches taller, ten shades lighter. But it is my face that is the target of their attention, and my black-winged eyebrow.

When I lean over my soup and look at him steadily, my dark eyes sheltered by my Kahlo eyebrow, he sighs and says softly...

You have no idea the effect you have on me, Frida.

In the ensuing silence, I say to myself... you are wrong, gringo. I know precisely what effect I have on you.. What you don't know is the effect you have on me.

***

A month has passed and a new portrait of myself and my little Frida is nearly complete. In this painting, the child I've conceived in my mind (and hopefully soon in my womb) sits on my knee. We both wear white Mexican dresses, and she is an intense miniature of myself.

Peter Cunningham has settled in for an extended stay at Orlando's insistence (and my resistance. The frog prince and the peacock prince are too much at war in the heart of my loins).

Frida, it's unfair to lump me and my brother together as irresponsible players in life. Paul was Paul, and I am Peter. The gringo and I are on our daily walk out along the headlands. I do this walk every day when I'm finished working in my studio, and two weeks ago he asked if he could come with me, and since, it's become our routine.

And unnervingly, each day he has expressed increasing attraction and attachment to me, all verbal, and I won't let him near me.

Look gringo. your brother was a good-looking man, too bad he wasn't a good man. I have no reason to believe you're anything more than he was.

His next words come like a rogue wave...

Look Frida, I haven't been able to think about anything but you since I got here... you're the most interesting, most challenging woman I've ever known... I'm in love with you... I love you... I want to share my life with you. I want you to be my wife...

He has tears in his eyes. He has taken two steps toward me. Looking past him, as I try to muster my defenses, the ocean is approaching with sensuous swells... swells as inevitable as...

He steps closer and gently puts his hands on my back and pulls me against him.

He looks at me with his dazzling smile and lifts me off the ground. I put my arms around his neck and straddle him Pamé-Frida style. With an audible slurp I engulf him, and my Pamé shrieks are in rhythm with my savage contractions.

It is over in seconds.

We slump to the ground, and dazed, I think of the Pamé way of trapping monkeys.

A gourd is secured to a stake, with a hole in the end just big enough for the monkey to slide his hand in. A piece of tasty bait is pushed into the opening of the gourd. When the monkey reaches in, excitedly grabbing the bait, his fist is too big to pull out of the hole. For some reason, the part of the monkey's brain that wants the bait doesn't communicate with the part that wants his freedom, so he won't let go, and is captured and killed.

The question is, now that this gringo bait is offered to me, and I have excitedly grabbed it, will I be able to let it go, and keep my life.

***

What?

This is my stunned response to one more of Hanna 's venomous verbal arrows.

Peter Cunningham and I are fucking... have been since a week after he got here.

I quell my flood of fury because I want more information. Does Hanna know about the gringo and me?

I ask with calm objectivity... But Hanna, what about Klaus?

She ignores my question and instead fills my stunned silence with her flippancy, the cadence of her German accent becoming more and more militant.

Look, how could I resist? He's beautiful. Why should I resist? From the start, it was, Hanna, you're the most interesting woman I've ever met... Hanna, I can't think about anything but you... Hanna, I'm in love with you.

And one night he made an amusing slip... he was carefully examining my nipples and he murmured something about the similarity to yours (we were both pretty stoned). Then he told me about the time you and he had sex at some wild party years ago, when you thought he was his brother and a little dalliance his brother agreed to, to keep Peter quiet after he found out about Susan, was that her name? The one his brother dumped you for?

In seconds I have reverted to such an ancestral state that I have forgotten all English words, so there's nothing more I can say to Hanna.

I leave her in her cold bemusement.

***

Frida darling...?

The gringo is behind me, and I know he is standing with his large hardness gleaming in the late Pacific sun, a stance I once told him was Greek-like and turned me on.

I have my back to him and am covered with a Pamé ceremonial robe I rarely wear. It covers my head and reaches to the ground, but is open in the front.

I turn and as I do, I let my robe drop to the ground.

His face is as white as the marble sculpture he mimes. His eyelids have drooped limply and he gasps for breath.

I am in my yellow power stripes. My hawk bones vibrate rapidly from the motion of my turning, held in place by my angry, hard nipples.

I open my mouth to let forth three piercing shrieks, baring my bright blue teeth.

He slumps to the ground, half-sitting.

In two quick steps. I am kneeling over him, holding his thick serpent in both hands. It is trying to escape, but to no avail. and I know the Pamé ritual well. the antidote to the Mexican rattlesnake that has unleashed its venom.

I stretch it between my strong hands and I hiss... if you and your snake are here an hour from now, I will kill you as I killed your vile clone and I will chomp this ugly viper to bits. I stand over him, glaring, my blue teeth gleaming ghoulishly.

He half stumbles, half runs toward the mansion, leaving his clothes behind.

When he is out of sight, I kneel to the ground and cry. I cry for myself and I cry for Orlando, and I cry for the baby Frida I know is inside of me, whose father is now an ominous unknown.

Two months have passed and the gringo is gone. He took my warning literally and was out of the gate of Orlando's estate in forty-five minutes, on foot.

Before he left, in one more virulent deed, after thanking Orlando for his hospitality, he told him what connoisseur's sex he had had with me.

Afterward, in telling me about it, Orlando shook his head and said...

You know you won't find that kind of malevolence in the world of nature. Down at the river, one creature may eat another, or attack another to protect its nest, but no creature would set out to render arbitrary hurt on the spirit of another. This is why I prefer the river to the arena of man.

Orlando has tears in his eyes as he says this, and he turns so I won't see them.

To his turned back, I say softly...

I know now that a new Frida is inside of me, and I don't know who the father is... what shall I do, Orlando?

There is a long silence while the frog prince breathes so deeply, I can see his jowls swell and empty from where I stand.

Finally, he turns, and with all the conviction of his considerable power in life says...

The new Frida will be born and we will love her. Who the father is, is of secondary importance.

Never has the frog prince seemed so princely. All three of us agree... grandmother Frida of the past, the Frida of the future, and the Frida of the present.

Orlando senses this, and says...

You're quite a constellation of Kahlo's, aren't you, my dear? As I smile, Frida past hums a little Mexican folk tune, and Frida future does a tiny precocious dance.

A half-year has passed, with the mansion as tranquil now as the summer days that surround us.

My belly has swelled and I am constantly in my studio, drawing my ever-changing shape.

There are one dozen drawings in Frida's diary documenting her changing shape, finally culminating in a belly with little appendages of arms and legs and a small head. This was fourteen-year-old Frida's picture of her pregnancy.

I have done the same... ten are finished, and I have two to go.

**

Hanna, on the other hand, is full to bursting (her baby is due any day), and she's taken to walking around the mansion nude, to the distress of Klaus and Orlando.

She has again shaved her head, and with the provenance of her baby a mystery, there is an ominous air in recent days at Pelican Reach.

Klaus has said, as Orlando said to me, that who the father is, is not an issue to him. But the question is, will it be an issue to Hanna?

Her breasts have swelled with her belly, and she often wears her osprey bones as she patrols the hallways of the mansion, naked, with her heavy-footed slap, slap, slap, slap.

**

Hanna's low moans increase in intensity as she looks down, squatting down, bearing down... waiting.

Hanna is in labor and she has asked Klaus and me to be in the room, and we each hold an arm, supporting her in her squatting position on the bed.

Hans is slowly circling us, dipping and rising to her soft rhythm as she summons forth her sibling with her flute, while eyeing the whole event with wary curiosity.

Hanna suddenly releases a great cascade of warm water that drenches Klaus and me, and begins bearing down with an expression of militant will. She seems possessed with the need to expel this baby as swiftly as possible.

As a result, it is a long, drawn out affair, Hanna cursing in German, her forehead beaded with sweat, her strong body in contortions of pain.

The baby seems as determined to stay safe inside as Hanna is to evict it. It is a battle of Germanic wills.

Two hours later, the crown of a dark-haired head reluctantly appears. Then surrendering an inch at a time, first a perfect ear, then a jaw, then the top of a shoulder, all the time Hanna howling who knows what in German (Klaus is cringing at what he hears).

Eleven hours later, we have cleaned off the bloody mucous as I've watched the Pamé women do, and lying before us is a perfectly beautiful boy who seems to be looking up warily at his admiring audience.

By the end of the week, however, we know that this baby is thoroughly blind.

***

All through the night, Hans had continued to play her flute, sometimes so soft it was barely audible.

We have a discussion with Hanna about the baby's father, initiated by her, during which she finally says...

Who cares? In any event the baby's name is Johann, a fine, old, prevailing German name, and he is the real embodiment of my dear dead twin, and I'm going to take Johann and Hans and leave this place.

When Hanna says this, Hans stops playing and stares at her.

The next morning Hans is gone from the mansion without a trace.

A week has passed... a week of intense searching involving every law enforcement agency in northern California, and still there is no sign of Hans.

In the meantime, doctors who examined the baby can find no physiological cause for his blindness, and they are puzzled. Hanna has slipped into her coldest Prussian mode. She seems only interested enough in her baby to feed him and give him minimal maternal attention. Her concern for Hans comes and goes.

Klaus is devastated by it all.

***

A month later I have finished my last drawing to document my ripe rotundity. I am fascinated by my belly, by my great ballooning form.

I stand and look in the mirror at my darkness and my lightness... my black hair parted above my black-winged eyebrow, above my slight shadow of black mustache, above my dark brown nipples, above my shiny black triangle covering the vestibule for the coming event. And lightness lives in my swelled, taut, luminous belly, which has within its own source of radiance.

***

Orlando darling, it's as though we're all under water in here.

We are in the deep-green room with the three Kahlo paintings on the wall. Grandmother will witness the bearing of the new Frida Kahlo.

Light is softly reflecting on the walls from the illuminated pool outside. Orlando and I both wanted the birth to happen close to where we first made love. I think believing it will somehow reflect the genetic makeup of my baby... our baby.

Orlando has said that we won't have any tests afterward to determine fatherhood. He has said repeatedly that we'll know who she came from when she's born. Then always adds... but that doesn't really matter, does it?

A bed has been moved into this room, and Orlando holds me from one side and dear loyal Klaus on the other, as I squat and strain with every last vestige of the artist within me to produce my portrait in flesh and blood.

As my contractions build, my water is released and rushes across the bed, and onto the floor around us it offers aquatic song to our underwater room.

I am flooded with artist's euphoria and I dilate with large generosity, inviting little Frida out into our world of love.

Sweating profusely and looking down, I see through the filmy fluid a pale blond head emerges, with a classically beautiful face, and under a dark winged eyebrow, luminous pale blue eyes looking directly into mine as though to gauge my response to her, and looking toward Orlando as though to apologize.

This little Botticelli version of Frida Kahlo continues her swim into the gentle hands of Orlando. I know that he is seeing a minute Peter Cunningham squirming in his unjudging hands, but only the slightest shadow crosses his face.

We clean up this little Frida, and taking inventory, begin to count her fingers, one, two, three, four, five, one, two, three, four, five... and her toes, one... two... three...

Suddenly Orlando stands and his frog prince jowls are ballooning and deflating and ballooning and deflating, making tender moist gurgling sounds as he holds up howling Frida against the window light so we can all see the pale, lovely translucent green webbing between her toes.

***

The mix of mood in the mansion these days ranges from the bliss we feel at baby Frida to the angry ambivalence Hanna feels toward baby Johann to our collective despair at the disappearance of Hans.

Klaus has withdrawn and I don't know what, if anything, now goes on between him and Hanna. He wants to believe the baby is his, but Hanna has said to him... what does it matter, my womb was polluted by Stoller... but at least my brother now has a proper body to re-exist in with a cock and balls.

We are all thankful that little Hans is not present to hear this.

***

Her face makes up for her feet...

This is Orlando's comment as he holds little Frida close to look at her carefully, as he does several times a day.

Frida reaches a tiny finger toward his wide frog prince mouth as though to point out the reason for her feet.

And her face is exquisite, with her gold hair, one dark winged Kahlo eyebrow, and clear cobalt eyes. So are her feet... they're just not like the feet of others.

And anyway, isn't the esthetics of appearance an arbitrary matter? I mean, just look at glorious Orlando.

***

Three months have passed and baby Johann's blindness is still a total mystery, and Klaus comes to Orlando and me one morning with his plan...

I'm leaving Pelican Reach to search for Hans. I owe her that, for she gave me back my vision. But I also believe the key to my baby's blindness lies with Hans. I could sense terrible conflict within her at the time of Hanna's birthing and I believe her powers... her strange omnipotence was confused and resulted in this terrible mistake... this blindness of our baby.

Orlando immediately agrees and offers to cover the expenses.

***

The morning Klaus leaves, there is sadness all around. He has been in many ways the conscience of Pelican Reach, the forgiving conscience.

How sad Hanna is, is hard to fathom. She holds Klaus for a long time, but her mind seems to be elsewhere, scheming some new scenario, which is precisely what we find in two days, when she leaves a note... a classic Hanna communique...

Johann and I have left.

Four

Orlando, it's another card from Klaus!

I hand Orlando the heavy reddish-brown card that I immediately eyed in the stack of mail Marie had brought in.

This is the third message we've received from Klaus in the five years he's been gone. Like the others, it is on beautiful hand-made paper, and is just as concise...

We are returning to Pelican Reach.

***

The first card we received, one year after Klaus had left read...

I have found Hans and she is fine.

***

The second card we received a year later... Johann is with us and he can see.

***

When we received Klaus's first card four years ago, we waited for further word, but none came. We considered trying to find them, but Orlando decided to let Klaus make his own decisions about the whole situation. We knew Hans was safe and that she was closer to Klaus than anyone, and probably still fearful of Hanna finding her and forcibly taking her back.

When we got the second card three years ago, we assumed that Klaus had been in touch with Hanna. Again, we expected further word and none came.

And now they are returning. Hans is seventeen, Johann is five, and Klaus is well into his sixties.

Orlando says with his usual acuity...

You know Frida, no matter what history of the past five years we imagine for them, it will seem bland compared to the reality.

***

For our part, for the past five years, Orlando and little Frida and I have been living a life of unhampered happiness. I have made hundreds of drawings and paintings of my three-muse family. Orlando has acquired dozens of major works to extend his collections (including two more of Grandmother's paintings). Little Frida has evolved precociously into a quintessential namesake. From the start, she was making urgent self-portraits (her first drawing was a heavy black horizontal line, with a dip in the middle).

She is also a true daughter of Orlando. She has taken to frog-kicking through the river waters and has already been graced with a gift of anchovies by the current Pelican prince. She even swallowed one, wriggling with revulsion. And unlike either of us, she is light-footed and light-hearted and prances about like a small ballerina.

Orlando and I have discussed several times this gift of untainted bliss, and if we speculate on what could threaten it, it is always Hanna's name that arises as though from some inferno in the cellar of the mansion.

***

They're here...!

Little Frida has dashed into the library, where Orlando and I have been sipping gin and watching the ocean while awaiting the three wanderers. She is as excited as we are since we've talked so much about Klaus and Hans and Johann. And since they all left before she was a month old, she has had to create her own image of them, and her imagination is as vivid as her bright expression tonight, punctuated by the only dark in her vivid lightness... her Frida Kahlo eyebrow doing gymnastics in nervous anticipation.

***

First through the doorway is Johann, self-possessed with a formal posture like Klaus's. Shyness comes and goes as he looks at me, at little Frida, and at Orlando, whose frog prince face brings a look of wonder to his eyes, in spite of the forewarning I'm sure he's received from Klaus.

He gives us each a slight genteel bow as he puts out his hand and says... Hello, I'm Johann.

When he stands before little Frida, her winged eyebrow is so active it seems about to lift her off the floor.

Next is Hans, and regardless of how many times I've told myself that she is no longer a twelve-year-old girl, I'm not prepared for what I see.

This almost eighteen-year-old young woman moves across the room in a ballet arabesque so graceful, her childhood limp seems forgotten. But in fact, it is still there, the dip and swing, but now it's an act of art.

Her face has the refined perfection of a Flemish Madonna.

And the coloring... rich, thick gold hair and pale blue introspective eyes.

She still drools, but attends to it consistently, with a quick movement of her delicate fingers.

She is taller than I expected, slightly more so than I. Her body is womanly, with ample breasts and hips.

She has the same sage, slightly ominous look about her... ageless and shaman-like.

Around her neck she wears a woven cord looped through a packet of tan, hand-made paper that rests against her breasts. In her hand is a red, felt-tip pen.

She stands before me looking steadily into my eyes for a long moment, and the room is still. Then she writes quickly on the paper, tears it loose, and hands it to me, still watching me intensely.

I read... to lifting up you my yes heart eyes are yes look love.

Before I can respond, Klaus has entered the room and says with unchanged calm dignity...

Hello everyone.

And then looking at me and nodding toward the paper in my hand says...

The words are rarely in the right order, but... he smiles... that's unessential, yes?

He appears to have a pride about Hans that even he can't conceal.

I look into Hans's timeless eyes and say... You, Hans... you lift my heart with love.

We embrace each other, and holding her fills me with her fragrance... a spicy, woodsy, animal-of-a-different species scent, deeply sensuous and enticing.

Klaus's hair is now very white, but long. His starched look is gone and his complexion is ruddy. All of them look like they've been living outside for the past five years.

When Klaus and I embrace each other, we each express our happiness at being together again.

Orlando envelopes Hans in his great soft, fleshy embrace.

Klaus and Orlando hug each other tight.

We all have tears in our eyes.

Little Frida has been watching all this intense expression of emotion and affection, and in the true style of her great grandmother, pulls Johann to her, giggling impishly.

For his part, Johann turns red as a poppy, but doesn't look displeased.

***

There is so much I want to ask Klaus (and Hans). Orlando too, but we sense they want to tell their story at their own pace and we wait for them.

At dinner, Little Frida has insisted that Johann sit next to her, and he shyly complies.

Klaus and Hans are each at one side of a corner of the table and Klaus leans slightly toward Hans as he eats, with his nostrils fluttering subtly.

The conversation is mostly about life here at the mansion. Soon the nomads are tired and go off to the three rooms Marie has readied for them.

***

Orlando and I have decided on a swim, to expend some of the nervous energy we have from suppressing our questions about Klaus and Hans and Johann.

Walking nude on the dark patio that leads to the pool, I pass. from a distance. the room that Hans has taken.

I glimpse bare flesh, and Grandmother Kahlo's irrepressible voyeurism is beyond my control.

I stealthily approach the window to see Hans leaning, naked, against the wall with her arms up and folded behind her head. Her body, which is visible only from the hips up, is curved out away from the wall in a graceful arc. Her head is turned toward me, but she is looking down, her eyes half closed in a trance-like reverie. A long string of ignored drool descends from her parted lower lip.

I am about to leave her to her strange solitary rapture, when I see that it isn't solitary at all.

Klaus's head ascends into view slowly. He moves his nose up over Hans's belly while sliding his hands up her hips. As Klaus carefully sniffs the surface of Hans, she in turn arcs her body further toward him, smiling dreamily.

When Klaus's face moves toward a full Hans breast, I turn to leave. At the same time, I feel guilt at spying, I'm also drawn to turn back and watch every juicy detail... Grandmother, as voyeur, is urging that... she can't believe we're leaving.

***

In the morning over coffee, Klaus wastes no time... Hans and I have been married... in a Klaruk ritual... Indians we've been living with... and we've adopted

Johann. (This of course makes Johann Hans's son as well as half-brother, but nothing is said of that.)

Klaus pauses to see how this information has settled with Orlando and me.

I don't know what my face expresses, but Grandmother thinks it all sounds tantalizing.

Orlando is impassive and unjudging, nodding to encourage Klaus to continue.

Hans is circling us at some distance, softly playing on her flute. She dips and swings gracefully in a choreography that is, as always, part of her music, eyeing each of us carefully to see our response to Klaus's words.

Her music now has a weight and maturity that goes way beyond her seventeen years, just as her music five years ago was beyond her twelve years.

Johann has been paying polite attention, but is soon led off by little Frida, who has no interest in long stories. As she leads him away by the hand, I can already see Grandmother's sense of adventure at play.

Klaus continues...

When I left here, five years ago, I felt I had already completed two lives.

When my wife and I went over the Berlin Wall, I should have been shot with her, and that life should have ended. It didn't, and my next life as a blind man could have ended because of this one...

Klaus nods toward Hans.

But it didn't, only the blindness ended.

So when I left here, I left as a man already graced with two lives... so this third life was a gift, and my responsibility was simply to allow it to be what it was intended to be. Intended by whom? I don't know, I'm not a believer in a higher being.

But I did feel the pull and power of Hans, and I believed that as long as I felt it, I would eventually find her. I also felt the pull of Johann.

So from the beginning I wandered, taking my direction from chance and intuition.

I traveled north and I traveled inland, taking rides wherever they were offered. I rode with logging truckers, ranchers, teenagers, migrant fruit pickers, affluent wine makers, farm wives, and Indians... young and old.

It was in the trailer of a Klaruk Indian that, after three months of travel, I was granted my clue to the whereabouts of Hans.

Whenever Klaus says Hans's name, he pauses to look over and confirm she's still here.

. This Indian, Lost Elk, seemed about my age. As we drove. we told each other our histories. I told him who I was looking for and why. He told me about leaving the Klaruk reservation years ago to work in a saw mill.

He lived in an old silver Airstream trailer, the rounded style that looked like a loaf of bread, home-baked out of aluminum. His trailer sat in a small clearing in a grove of enormous redwoods.

He invited me to stay the night because his daughter and granddaughter were coming down from the tribal lands the next day to visit him, and he wanted me to meet them. It was his granddaughter's birthday.

He slept on the sofa, and I slept on a green fake leather recliner. It was very pleasant there, surrounded by redwoods and with Lost Elk telling me the four-thousand-year history of the Klaruk people.

The next afternoon, his daughter, who seemed in her early twenties, arrived with her nine-year-old daughter. They, like Lost Elk, had long, black glossy hair, coal black eyes, and handsome angular features.

Lost Elk told me that he was forty-one and that Klaruk women married early.

The afternoon was awkward and self-conscious and would have been boring if not for an event that made my heart pound.

Among the birthday presents Lost Elk had given the girl was a cheap tin whistle, which she tooted on discordantly a couple of times, and then set aside.

But later in the afternoon, I heard softer, more melodic notes coming from the woods, and I walked out to investigate.

In a clearing, some distance from the trailer, the girl was walking in a circle and blowing on her whistle... but she wasn't walking... she was dipping and rising, dipping and rising, as though her left leg was shorter than the right.

When she heard me approach, she stopped and turned to face me, and there was a long string of drool suspended from her lip, which was being added to with pushes of her tongue as she looked at me absently.

I startled her with the urgency of my questions...

Where did you learn to walk like that? Limp like that? Drool like that?

I was on my knees in front of her, holding her arms.

The girl looked alarmed. She turned her head toward the trailer and then back to me. She opened her mouth as though to speak, but then her mother was calling to her and coming through the woods.

I asked her again where she had learned that limp, and now her expression was a child's look of stubborn secrecy.

Her mother was at the clearing and the girl was struggling to free herself from me, and her mother was shouting...

Let go of her! What are you doing to her?

***

It took an hour of Lost Elk's reasoning with his daughter and confirmation from his granddaughter that I had in fact done nothing to her in order to escape being reported for child molestation.

Lost Elk's family left then, quite abruptly, without looking in my direction again.

I tried to get information from Lost Elk, but he kept repeating that he hadn't been on the reservation for five years, and that lots of things happened there that would seem strange to a white man.

Even his description of the location of the reservation was vague...

There are tribes that are only tributaries to the main tribe, and they live on smaller rivers that are tributaries to the main river, the Hoyak. And there are places where no non-Klaruk has ever been or ever will be.

I tell Lost Elk that I'm sure that Hans is there and that I'm going to find her.

He responds soberly...

If I were a white man, I wouldn't go into those tribal lands.

***

While Klaus has been telling about his encounter with Lost Elk. we have all been spellbound, including Hans, and I wonder if she's hearing this part of the story for the first time.

Orlando stands, stretches, and says...

Let's walk the beach.

***

Down by the water, our outing is accompanied by swooping gulls, sprinting sandpipers, and the black buzzards picking at the carcasses of ducks who have dropped out of life's race.

It is warm and cool at the same time, as it often is down here... the sun versus the ocean breeze and the dry sand versus the wet. This makes me think of Hanna, how she could switch from hot to cold in an instant, and how my thoughts of her today come like a cold slice of air from the sea to assault our happy gathering.

As we walk the beach, little Frida and Johann dash out after receding waves and back in ahead of them like sandpipers, afflicted with giggling.

Hans is walking in front of me, and I notice in the sand the cursive marks of her limp, like calligraphy whose message will never be known.

Orlando, alongside me, walks unsteadily, as usual, his great mass awkwardly balanced on small lower legs. He stares out to sea.

I don't yet know what Orlando thinks of what Klaus has told us. When I told him what I saw through Hans's bedroom window he said nothing, but his large eyes swelled slightly and his frog prince jowls expanded and contracted while he digested my report.

Klaus is as upright as ever and he stares straight ahead as he continues his story...

It took three days of assorted rides to get to the outer boundaries of the Klaruks. I was very far north, and well inland from the sea.

The terrain was hilly, heavily forested, and wild. The wide Hoyak River ran through the middle of the tribal lands, and as Lost Elk said, there were a number of smaller rivers feeding into it.

This was information I gleaned from an outfitter five miles downriver from the Klaruks. I rented a canoe, tent and sleeping bag from this man.

He was very inquisitive about my plan and I was very vague in my answers. He was skeptical about my heading upriver.

I wouldn't go more than three or four miles, he said.

I paid him cash and he asked for what seemed like a large deposit for his canoe and equipment. I think he never expected to see me again.

I had a map, and pointing to where a bridge spanned the Hoyak River, he said... I wouldn't go east of here.

***

Because I was paddling upriver, it took the whole day, resting twice, to reach the bridge of warning. It was dusk by then, and I decided to wait until dark to paddle into the Klaruk lands.

It was the night of a new moon, which I took as an auspicious beginning, and I was reassured by the darkness it offered. In the pitch black I pushed off from the shore, and paddling as quietly as possible, I passed under the bridge with trepidation.

I had no plan... I was again following my intuition. I hoped only to hear Hans's playing at some point, or, less likely, to catch a glimpse of her. But what I didn't expect was to catch a whiff of her, and that is what happened.

Four hours into the tribal lands, I noticed a smaller river, a wide stream really, flowing into the Hoyak. I paddled up this stream for a half an hour or so, and at a low grassy spot I pulled the canoe up on shore.

It was perfectly still. I unrolled my sleeping bag and lay back, exhausted from paddling, and within minutes dozed off. With my eyes closed my sense of smell is always more acute, because then I revert back to a dependence on other senses, as when I was blind.

I woke later to a feeling of sweet melancholy and lay in a dream-like trance while trying to trace the source of my feelings.

It was then that I recognized the unique fragrance of Hans wafting down the slope of forest behind me.

You know, when I was blind, I could recognize any of you, even from a distance.

This scent of Hans was just a nuance, and was mixing with the moist fragrance of the ferns it was moving through, as though on its way to this stream, and to the river, and to the ocean, and down the coast to Pelican Reach, as if calling out to me but not knowing I was so close.

As Klaus finishes saying this, Hans stops in front of us and, in one of the rare playful gestures I've ever seen from her, presses her nose against her forearm and raises her eyebrows as though in response to her own scent.

It is a gesture so endearing and amusing that we all laugh, including Hans. The children run back to see what they're missing.

Johann nuzzles himself between Klaus and Hans, and seeing this, little Frida does the same between Orlando and me. And here we are, our two odd family clusters facing each other. As we each look from one to the other, I sense that they, like I, are re-screening the movie of all that's transpired since I arrived at Pelican Reach six years ago.

On our way back down the beach to the mansion, Klaus continues his story...

I stood upright in the grove of trees surrounding me and decided to literally follow my nose. I started up the incline, trying to make no more noise that I did in the canoe. I walked for an hour or so and reached a plateau. On the other side of a clearing, I could see lights. I was now extremely fatigued and in need of sleep, so I walked into the woods at the edge of the clearing and up a slope to a fallen tree. Behind this tree I lay down, and again was asleep in minutes.

Once more my sleep was disrupted by Hans. This time it was her music, and it came just at dawn. I opened my eyes and the sky above me was crimson and Han's playing was the musical equivalent of the color of that sky.

I looked over the log I lay behind, and down below, the sun was slanting onto a grassy field, turning the night dew to a rising white mist. Through this mist a line of Indians was moving snake-like and each was dipping down on his (or her) left leg in unison, and back up again, and each was suspending a string of spittle from the corner of his or her mouth.

At the head of the procession was Hans, blowing forcefully into her flute, playing a strange and moving improvisation that so embodied the whole quality of the morning, it seemed as though she had ordered it all up.

The entourage of Indians included everyone, old and young, male and female. There was a man who must have been close to a hundred, and he had the Hans limp down as though she'd been tutoring him for years. A three- or four-year-old girl was equally skilled in her uneven walk.

All the Indians were dressed in ordinary clothes... jeans, T-shirts, cotton dresses, sneakers, baseball caps. This could have been any gathering in northern California... but it wasn't... it was this one's gathering.

Klaus again puts his hand affectionately on Hans's cheek, and Hans smiles shyly, shy at the attention, but not, I sense, shy about her powers.

We are now walking up the slope to the terrace of the mansion. Once inside, we all go off for a siesta before dinner.

***

What do you think Orlando?

We are lying together on our spacious frog prince bed. The translucent curtains that diffuse the late sun seem like billows of white mist, and I am recreating in my mind the image of Hans leading the Indians in their dawn choreography.

Orlando is silently pondering my question. Finally he says...

I really don't know what to think. Klaus is, of course, a changed man from when he left here. But Hans... she is a woman now... and a bit of magic. I have to say I'm in awe of her, and I don't quite know what to expect. Her presence gives Pelican Reach the feeling that anything could happen here. It's a little frightening. And there's still so much we don't know... five years' worth. And what about Hanna?

As if to eclipse all thoughts of those five years, Orlando makes love to me in his slow and easy aqueous manner as though our mattress is a remote marsh and we have a whole mating season before us in this hour before dinner.

***

At dinner, Klaus continues his story, after we have taken a few minutes to help Orlando's mother understand that the Hans before her is indeed the same Hans as five years ago. (Madame Pettingill has held up well physically and slipped only a little more mentally.) She had kept repeating...

Oh no, this woman is too big to be little Hans (and she is right).

Klaus looks at each of us while going on with his story... At the close of Han's paean to the new day, she led the Indians into a spiral, which in the end was tightly wound around her as she sent forth one last high trill.

The sun now shone bright on the gathering of dancers, like the stage lights fully up at the close of a performance.

When Hans's last notes had left the clearing, everyone but Hans squatted on the ground as though in deference to her, which she took as natural, and if it were expected.

After a few moments the Indians stood and silently walked off in various directions. Then a powerfully built middle-aged Indian approached Hans, and walking beside him was Lost Elk's granddaughter.

They huddled together for a few moments and then turned and walked in my direction. I lay back down behind the log, giving them time to leave the clearing.

But soon I heard footsteps close by and I looked up to see the three of them standing on the other side of the log staring down at me.

The man looked severe. Lost Elk's granddaughter looked amazed. And Hans... Hans looked as triumphant as the day she restored my sight.

As Klaus says this, he looks at Hans, who is again wearing the same glowing expression as when she led Klaus back from his vision-restoring plunge five years ago.

Watching Hans, Klaus continues...

Exactly what preceded my being there, I'll never know, but here is what I've pieced together over the past few years with the help of Hans' written words...

***

When Hans left here that morning, five years ago, she walked along the bank of the river until she got to the bridge, then climbed up to the highway and hitched a ride north. Her reason for leaving was fear of Hanna taking her away with her, probably to Germany.

Once on the road, she had no trouble getting rides because she was so intriguing, and, as she said, she smiled a lot.

The second day, her last ride was with an Indian woman who left her off before she turned into the Klaruk lands. After waiting on the highway until dark with no new ride, Hans walked into the Indian lands and then up a foot path through huge redwoods until she was exhausted.

When she woke, the color of the sky inspired a flute sonata.

That same night, the chief of one of the tribes (the muscular man who found me behind the tree, named Bear Claw) dreamed that he would find a bird meant to be his wife.

When he heard Han's playing in the morning, he walked until he found her in the woods. She was playing a soft melodic tremolo, and Bear Claw, in the conviction of his dream, saw a beautiful exotic bird enveloped in white mist sitting where Hans was playing.

When he finally stood before her and saw this beautiful girl, he was convinced of the truth of his dream. He put out his hand and said...

I am Bear Claw, chief of my tribe... are you to be my wife?

Hans thought this amusing and smiled, taking Bear Claw's hand.

Klaruk girls marry as early as twelve or thirteen, so Bear Claw saw before him not a child, but his young bride-to-be, sent by the Indian god of union in his dream.

He took her back to the village and everyone made a huge fuss over her, because not only was she to be their chief's wife, but she was a kind of goddess... goddess of dawn, they decided.

One week after her arrival, during which she played a new improvisation each morning, as prelude to the coming day, a wedding ceremony was to take place.

The elder women of the tribe washed and anointed Hans with herbal potions meant to make her fertile. When they saw her nipples, Hans obligingly put in her snowy egret bones and the Klaruks were more convinced than ever that she had come to Bear Claw as a sacred bird presence.

The night of the wedding ceremony, when the women wanted to shave Hans's pubis as a show of invitation to Bear Claw, Hans finally understood what was to take place and what was expected of her.

She shook her head no, and seeing the severe reaction of the Klaruk women, and even more so of Bear Claw, Hans mimed out her explanation. She was, she conveyed, promised to another man, who was coming to get her.

The Klaruks assumed that Hans was promised by the gods to another man, and their awe of Hans forced them to accept her rejection of Bear Claw.

However, they were disgruntled and left her alone that night. Hans did not play her paean until dawn, and it so happened that a freak storm moved into the river valley, complete with howling winds and pellets of hail.

When the storm passed, and the sun came out, creating columns of white mist to rise from the puddles in the clearing, Hans limped out and began to play her flute. One by one the Klaruks came out to line up behind her, and to copy her limp as she walked. In the end, when she stopped playing, they all squatted down around her, and that was when the whole meandering dawn ritual began.

So, by the time I appeared, I was already invested with power because I was presumably sent by the same gods who sent Hans... to be her husband.

***

Hans wanted to stay with the Klaruks because she thought it was the only place she'd be safe from Hanna returning to take her away. Besides, it was beautiful and serene here, and Hans came to like the people of the village, as did I.

The Klaruks, however, insisted that Hans and I marry (believing that if we didn't, the gods that conceived of our union would be provoked). So we were married by the Klaruks four-and-a-half years ago. It was a short, intense ceremony at dawn. Afterward, we moved into one of the cedar plank lodges, and lived happily and chastely together.

Hans played her flute every day for hours, and her music became more moving and beautiful by the day.

I had made paper by hand in Germany early in my life, and I began to do that again. It was that paper Hans believed she could learn to write on, and she did.

We started by my pointing to an object, writing out the word, and Hans copying what I wrote. I mimed out the meaning of abstract words, wrote them down, and Hans would do the same. Then I combined simple words. and then more complex words.

We spent hours every day at this, and eventually Hans was conveying ideas by mixing words in unusual combinations.

It fascinated her and she wrote that it was like playing her flute... improvising.

Orlando looks at Klaus with his great intense eyes and says with some impatience...

Klaus, how and where did you find Johann, and how did he regain his sight?

Klaus answers...

One of the Klaruk women, who had left the tribal lands for a year, returned with news of Johann and Hanna.

This woman had worked in a state agency for abandoned children. The only reason she mentioned Hanna and Johann was because they were so striking... Hanna with her shaved head and nose loops, and Johann, a blind and stoic one-year-old.

Hanna wanted to give up Johann because she couldn't cope with a blind child. The agency said she couldn't, because she wasn't a resident of the state or even a US citizen.

So Hanna acted in her usual decisive Germanic manner and the next day simply left Johann in the corridor outside the agency office with this note...

The father is either Heinrich Stoller or Klaus Zimmer.

***

So Hans and I made a ten-hour bus trip to the agency. I identified myself as Klaus Zimmer, and they gladly gave me Johann.

When we returned to the Klaruk lands, Johann was immediately embraced by everyone, and we settled him into our cedar lodge. We were like a small family now. So much so that the Klaruks insisted we have a ceremony to grant Johann the status of son to Hans and me.

And we did that in another intense ritual at dawn.

This ceremony unfolded in two stages. The first took place at dawn, with Hans and Johann and I huddled together in the center of the clearing, mist rising around us, and the whole tribal village in a large loose circle surrounding us.

At the slow beat of a drum made from the skin of a matriarchal moose, the Klaruks, a step at a time, approached us until the circle was tight, and then came closer, until the circle was many Indians deep and finally we were pressed against by the whole village in a monolithic mass of Klaruks. This was meant to make Johann a son of the village. Each of the Indians was imbued with a different scent, ranging from various plants to excretions of the glands of the different animals of the area. The combination of the odors, sweet and spicy and musky, was literally intoxicating. As Hans and I held Johann between us, I noticed his nostrils flutter with interest. He was turning his small head abruptly from one scent to another, and even leaning his face forward with eyebrows raised, as though to see what he was smelling.

Then we were taken from the clearing to a small circular sweat lodge, which had been heating up for hours. The interior was almost totally dark, with just one small oil lamp behind us.

We took off our clothes and again sat close together, barely able to see each other. Hans and I sat facing each other, our knees touching. We passed Johann back and forth between us one hundred times. the count pounded out by another drum outside.

We were perspiring profusely and the only scent in the close circular space was our own, each distinct, but each melding with the others to form the complex fragrance of family... our family.

When I would receive little Johann, he would hold me tight, pressing his wet face against my wet neck or chest, and then do the same with Hans.

Johann became very tired, and, as he did, all wariness seemed to leave him. He seemed only aware of our aura of redolence.

Now as he was passed back and forth between us, it was his nose he pressed against us, and again he began to raise his eyebrows and turn his head up as though to try and see our smell.

When the drumbeats ended, Hans and I held Johann silently between us, and in his trance-like delirium, he slowly turned his head from one of us to the other, leaning forward, his nostrils dilating, and squinting, as though he felt there had to be another dimension to this phenomenon.

It was then I reached behind me for the oil lamp. I moved it toward Johann. His squint seemed to deepen, and when I moved the lamp toward my face, he turned his head to follow it.

I held the lamp close to my face and remained still. Johann opened his nostrils and leaned toward me breathing rapidly. He turned his eyes up to mine and it was as though a delicate film evaporated and those very eyes I had looked into a thousand times for some response were now looking into mine with awe and bewilderment.

***

When Klaus says this, Johann, who is sitting next to him, turns to Klaus and smiling impishly, moves his face close and opens his eyes wide. We all laugh, but Klaus has tears in his eyes.

***

Klaus has promised to tell us about Hanna the next morning, but he doesn't get a chance. She appears on the terrace while we're having our coffee.

Hans is so immobilized she lets a string of drool slowly descend to the table.

Klaus turns ashen.

Orlando's jowls and eyes are enormous.

Johann is alarmed by everyone's response, but puzzled, since he's never seen his mother.

Little Frida's eyebrow wing is as high as it will go, and stays there.

Even after all I've been through with Hanna, her presence still sends a chill into my spine.

***

For her part, Hanna calmly observes us all with amusement.

When she walked onto the terrace all talk ceased, and no one has offered anything to fill the silence.

In this surreal absence of sound, more like a dream than an overcast morning at Pelican Reach, I observe Hanna...

***

Her hair is shiny and long and tied once in the back with a soft lavender velvet ribbon. She has small, delicate wildflowers tucked randomly into her hair.

Her dress is white silk, beautifully fitted, and hangs on her with elegance.

She looks like a bride.

***

Hanna breaks the silence...

I was married at dawn... romantic, yes? To Peter Cunningham. I've come for my son.

Five

I am Frida Kahlo IV.

My mother, also Frida Kahlo, has granted me permission to continue and conclude this narrative.

I am eighteen years old, and it is thirteen years since Hanna appeared in her silk wedding dress to take Johann away from Pelican Reach. And more devastatingly, away from me.. I say devastatingly, not because I had a five-year-old's crush on Johann (although it's true I did) but because he and I were born within a month of each other, we were inseparable at the age of five, and we were meant to spend our lives together... that is what I believed.

***

And, in true Kahlo fashion, I have within me a dual destiny I have never questioned...

Destiny number one...

To become a world-class dancer in a premier company, and I am that, with the Royal Stockholm Ballet.

Destiny number two...

To find Johann and make him mine, in the true Frida/Diego, Frida/Orlando style.

That is yet to come. I haven't even found him yet.

However, I have recently been told that he lives in Leipzig. Germany, with his parents, Hanna and Peter.

This word I received from my father, Orlando, whose wonderful webbing also graces my feet and facilitates my pointe positions.

In appearance, that is the only detail I've inherited from him... probably a good thing, lovable frog prince that he is. From my mother, all I inherited is her (and great-grandmother's) one dark-winged eyebrow, which on my face seems like mischievous graffiti on a metro billboard.

I have lightness in every sense that my mother doesn't. My hair is citron blond, my skin is alabaster white, my eyes are cerulean blue.

I am three inches taller than she, and my slightness, abetted by dance, give the impression I'm about to levitate at any moment... while my mother is without question, a woman of the earth.

As I say, what we have in common is the Kahlo eyebrow, of which I'm proud and vain, and which when people meet me makes them stare. And when I dance, it seems like the partner in my pas de deux.

***

When Hanna came for Johann, thirteen years ago, Klaus, with the help of Orlando's lawyers, demanded DNA testing so he could prove he was the father of Johann, and keep him. The tests were done, and alas, proved that Klaus was not the father, which cleared the way for Hanna and her husband, Peter Cunningham, to leave for Germany with Johann, which they did.

And I have not seen or heard from Johann since. It hurt me that he didn't, in time (after all, he was only five when they left) try to contact me.

I would have let it go, if it weren't for my innate conviction that Johann was meant to be my prince (of whatever mode). I believed it because it all began (we both began) at magical Pelican Reach.

***

Within a year of Johann's abduction (I still believed he wanted to stay with me), I began to lope through the corridors of the mansion with leaps and pirouettes, and soon announced I wanted to be a dancer.

I began to listen to ballet music and watch films of dance of all kinds. I was so insistent and so intense that my parents arranged for me to have a dance tutor.

Madame Oblimakov had retired to the north coast of California. She had been a principal dancer with the Russian Ballet, and after that, a famous dance teacher in New York.

She was eighty-two when she came to the mansion as a favor to her old friend Orlando, to observe his little blond prancing daughter.

They all thought it would be a matter of one cordial afternoon, and even my mother underestimated the force of a Frida Kahlo ambition.

As it turned out, I was taken to Madame Oblimakov's house every day for a year, where in her living room, she would sit upright, both hands folded over the cane in front of her, barking out instruction to me in barely understandable English, while I moved around the room to the music of the pianist who accompanied us.

She did not do this as a favor to Orlando, or even for the money (a large amount, I suspect). She did it because, as she said early on... it is, I think, a very large talent in this very little body.

So, at the age of eight, I was enrolled at the prestigious New York School of Ballet, arranged through the iron will of Madame Oblimakov, their renowned teacher emeritus.

Klaus and Hans accompanied me to New York, and we all lived in an enormous apartment on Fifth Avenue overlooking Central Park, purchased by my father, the frog prince.

My mother would come and go many times during the year, as did Orlando.

Klaus and Hans were paid by my father to look after me, and they also made lives for themselves in the city.

***

Day after day, month after month, my life was consumed by dance. As rebellious relief from the strictness of my dance lessons (which I loved), I only broke the school rules in one way...

Starting when I was about ten, Hans and I performed together in some artsy downtown loft spaces. We would improvise back and forth, sometimes Hans starting with her flute and I following, and sometimes I starting with movements and Hans following with her music.

Back on the other coast, my mother became famous for her self-portraits, and she was approaching the status of my great grandmother... all of which fed my own motivation as an artist. I was not going to be the generation of Frida Kahlos that dissolved into anonymity.

**

In New York, I so concentrated my energies on dance that I had almost no social life outside of Klaus and Hans, and their friends who came to visit.

As a result, I've never had a boyfriend. This is due to my having set a very high standard for... let's call it romantic intimacy. This came about because I am a Frida Kahlo, and the Fridas before me (and often, within me) were such voyeurs... perhaps because, as painters, they were so visual.

You could say it was my curiosity for the exotic that began my high standards for erotic intimacy. It took the form of my crawling out of the window of my room at night onto our common Fifth Avenue balcony to peer under the blinds of Klaus's and Hans's bedroom window. It started when I was ten and continued for six years, until I left New York for Stockholm.

I could never see much at one time because of the ornate end board of their bed, and the chair by the window. What I could almost always see though was Hans's face, which always wore an expression of sublime ecstasy... eyes three-quarters closed, cheeks flushed, nostrils dilating, and her mouth overflowing with drool as though it were the sexual organ.

There were nights so intriguing I lay outside on the balcony with snow slowly covering me until I was a transfixed ogling ghost.

This night-time spying, combined with my day-time observation of their quiet joy with each other, has made me determined to have nothing less in my life.

And besides... I am saving myself for Johann.

***

So when I got word from my father that Johann and his parents were in Leipzig, I decided to go find him and bring him home... a classic, unequivocal Frida Kahlo scheme.

There was a two-week break in our performance schedule and I had a slight knee injury, so I could justify not staying in Stockholm to rehearse. My plan was to take a little holiday in Leipzig, an old center of Saxon culture, and just look around and ask around until there was some sign of Johann. I'd already checked for a Leipzig phone number and there wasn't one.

***

During the train ride from Stockholm, and the ferry ride across the Baltic, and another train ride to Leipzig, I thought of all the things that might have happened in Johann's life in these past thirteen years.

The one thing that seemed likely is that being just eighteen, he is probably a student, so I decided to make the university district of Leipzig the center of my search. If I stayed in that area and spent my days roaming that area, I would surely find him and when I found him my heart would do pirouettes.

***

I enjoyed three days of pleasant wanderings... pleasant because this small city is filled with young people, and pleasant because I continued to romantically re-imagine the meeting with my prince.

Then one afternoon, I did see Johann, but he didn't see me...

I was sitting at a large outdoor cafe having coffee. It was crowded with university students who were enjoying the boisterous freedom of their age, a freedom I never had, cloistered in my monastic world of dance.

In a slight pause in the cacophony around me, I heard... Johann!

Sabine?

Yes, love...

I stood immediately to look in the direction of the voices, and there he was, sitting at a small round table near the doorway to the cafe.

His beautiful face was rapt with anticipation of the approaching blond girl. I knew it was Johann even though I haven't seen him since he was five because the five-year-old Johann was still there in his face.

His hair was dark and neatly trimmed, his face lean, with sculpted cheek bones and chin, his mouth narrow and fine, as were his fingers. folded before him on the table.

The girl, Sabine, carried a violin case, and on the table by Johann's coffee was his violin case.

Sabine sat next to Johann and put her hand over his. They leaned forward and kissed.

The long-cloistered dancer within me sadly said... Let's go Frida...

But great grandmother Kahlo immediately countered that with...

Don't you dare leave... walk to the cafe doorway and stop to ask a question. See if he can see the five-year-old Frida in you.

So, I approached their table, my heart pounding and my hands shaking, and in what sounded like the frightened voice of a five-year-old girl, I said...

Excuse me, can you tell me how to get to the Bosehaus, you know, the Bach family home...? I see you're musicians, so you seemed the right people to ask...

I spoke to Johann, but glanced once toward Sabine.

Johann seemed startled by my voice and looked quickly at me, but his eyes didn't connect with mine... they were aimed slightly off to the right of me.

As I looked at the fine film over his eyes, I also saw the white cane hooked over the back of the chair I was standing by.

Sabine was the one to answer...

Ah, yes... if you go straight ahead three blocks, you will come to Burg Strasse, and there you should turn right and one block up you will see Thomaskirche, the church where Bach was choirmaster for twenty-seven years, and where he wrote most... of his... cantatas...

Sabine's nervous chatter finally faltered as she looked now in silence from me to Johann to me.

Tears were streaming down my cheeks as I watched Johann lean slightly toward me, his nostrils flared and his forehead furled with what I wanted to believe is the remembrance of a five-year-old boy in California.

Finally, it was all too excruciating to experience any longer, and thanking Sabine, I turned and left.

I was counting my steps and at five, as great grandmother had predicted, there was a youthful shout behind me...

Frida!

***

So, eyebrow... I hope you don't mind my calling you that. I used to call your mother that... anyway, it's the one distinctive thing about you.

This is Hanna commenting from her imperious position at the head of the long table in the elaborate dining room of the rococo mansion Peter Cunningham has purchased for his little family of three... soon to become four, when Johann and Sabine are married in four months.

It is one week since I first saw Johann at the cafe. He has insisted that I stay here at their home for the remainder of my holiday in Germany. Hanna readily agreed. She, it seems is the only one aware of my feelings for Johann, and she is taking her usual perverse pleasure in observing the suffering of a Frida Kahlo.

Hanna is now in her fifties, and has put on considerable weight. With her short-groomed hair and expensive bourgeois wardrobe, she is the perfect Frau Cunningham.

Peter Cunningham is silver-haired and vacuous, his huge inherited wealth long having sheltered him from any contact with real life.

He is still a collector of art though, and I am unnerved to find two self-portraits of great grandmother gracing the walls of one of the sitting rooms, and even more stunned to see one of my mother's paintings of herself and me from before I was conceived. It's a disturbing painting because she had of course painted me with all of her own darkness.

***

I have had only a few brief conversations with Johann alone. Between Sabine and Hanna. Johann has (it seems) been deliberately kept from me.

Finally, toward the end of my last week there, it was necessary for Johann to be guided to a rehearsal. Everyone else had to be somewhere else, so I had my one and only chance to ask all the questions of Johann I'd been saving.

As we walked down a quiet street, Johann holding my arm gently, was awaiting my first question...

Johann, where and what?

He smiled and immediately said...

I know Frida, I have all this information about your past thirteen years and you know nothing of mine.

This is true. At every meal there was a barrage of questions not only about me, but about my mother, Orlando, Klaus, and Hans.

I gave candid (and looking back at it now, naive) answers. And some of my answers produced intense interest from Hanna and Peter.

But on this day, alone with Johann, I only want to talk about him, hear about him.

The answer to what must be your first question, about my blindness... perhaps you never knew, Frida, but I was born blind, for reasons that were a mystery. And,

I was told, when I was one year old, I lived in an Indian village in northern California with Klaus and Hans, who were like my parents. Well, in a ritual in a sweat lodge with Hans and Klaus, my sight was magically restored.

But when my mother took me from Pelican Reach when I was five, it was so traumatic, because of Hans and Klaus, and you too, dear Frida. You know, I had a five-year-old's crush on you... more than that, I was in love with you. Silly, yes? I believed we were destined to spend our lives together.

I so wish I could see your face now, to see if that impish five-year-old is still there, somewhere.

At any rate, after we left, we lived in many different places. When, early on, I showed interest in music, Hanna and Peter arranged for violin lessons, starting when I was about eight. It relieved them that I could accomplish something in spite of my blindness.

We moved here two years ago because my violin teacher became first violinist with the Leipzig Symphony.

My mother was born here, and she decided this is where we would live for the time being. Peter always goes along with what Hanna wants.

Sabine then became a student of my teacher, which is how we met, and for the past year and a half, she's been my seeing-eye dog (Johann smiles) and in time, we...

I fill in for Johann's shyness... You became lovers.

Well, let's just say we became close, and we became engaged.

Silence.

Frida... ?

Yes.

May I feel your eyebrow... ? You know, I remember it.

Yes.

We stop on the sidewalk, and as people walk around us, Johann traces a finger slowly over my dark wing. He is standing close to me and I can see he is inhaling deep and I know he is breathing in my scent.

You know, Frida, I can remember your face as a five-year old, and I can re-member what you smelled like when we used to wrestle for something the other one didn't want to give up. You smelled like sweet pastry dough, and that's what I smelled two weeks ago at the cafe that first day. Isn't that incredible.

Yes Johann, it is.

I'm glad he can't see the tears streaming down my cheeks, but he surprises me...

Now you smell like wet pastry dough.

And at this Johann traces two fingers across my cheek and down over my trem-bling mouth.

I'm so sorry Frida.

This he says just before turning into the doorway of the concert hall, leaving me outside listening to the various instruments tuning up inside. His world... his and Sabine's world.

***

So, Frida IV, you have your nipples pierced too, yes?

This is Hanna, face flushed with red wine and stomach full of the red meat she's gorged herself on tonight. We're having dinner to honor my departure for Stockholm tomorrow morning.

This stops the conversation at the table, which was obviously Hanna's inten-tion. The talk was too full of good will.

Everyone... Johann, Sabine, Peter, Hanna, and a handsome young German ballet dancer who's been invited to round out the symmetry of couples... everyone turns to see what my response will be to this bit of Hanna enmity.

I take my time before I answer...

Yes Hanna, and I'm proud of my pierced nipples, as I'm proud of my Pamé heritage, which in due time will have its way...

I say this while looking steadily at Hanna. The room is silent.

Then I turn to face Johann (he senses this and he leans slightly toward me).

And Johann, the bones that pierce my nipples when I want to embody my Pamé power, they are the bones of a sandpiper, because the most joyful memory of Pelican Reach I have is you and I running in and out of the shallow beach waters like sandpipers with no worry in the world.

***

Late that night, there is a soft knock on my door. It is Johann and he asks to come in.

After apologizing for his mother's behavior at dinner, he asks if he can feel my sandpiper bones.

You know, Frida, only after you said that about the sandpipers did I remember that off and on over these thirteen years I've had many dreams of running in and out of those shallow ocean waters.

I go to my suitcase and unwrap the burnished white bones and hand them to Johann.

We both stand in silence while he runs his fingers over and around the smooth surfaces.

As he does this I remember my mother describing her first meeting with Hanna, when Hanna saw mother's pierced nipples and asked about them, and then, holding the hawk bones in her hand, said...

May I put them in?

Just as that memory moves through my mind, this son of Hanna says...

May I put them in? .

You have to use a little saliva, and they're meant to go in a little past halfway. with the thick end on the outside.

***

Ah, little Frida my dear... I'm so happy we're all together tonight.

It is Christmas Eve, three months since I left Leipzig to return to Stockholm, and this is my sweet father, Orlando, talking softly to me as he strokes my hair, his huge eyes glistening with emotion.

We are in Orlando's and mother's newly purchased country home on the outskirts of Stockholm, acquired so that when they come to see me, we can all be comfortably together.

This is a classic Swedish retreat for the well-to-do. It is constructed of great cedar logs, but is quite refined on the interior, white plaster meeting the old polished woodwork. It is filled with soft, embracing, over-stuffed couches and chairs and lovely rugs from around the world.

There are several sitting rooms, parlors, living rooms, and a library, many bedrooms, and a kitchen equipped with long, heavy tables, two large copper ovens, and glass-fronted cabinets filled with Swedish glass and dishes.

***

Tonight is to be a celebration dinner... three nights ago, I had my first solo performance with the Stockholm Royal Ballet. It was a holiday gala, and the guest orchestra was the Leipzig Symphony... with both Johann and Sabine playing in the second violin section.

As a result, all the people of Pelican Reach are here in Stockholm at the same time... Orlando and my mother, and also Hans and Klaus, and, as we recently discovered, Johann and Sabine, and Hanna and Peter.

So, Orlando, in a gesture of holiday generosity and reconciliation, invited everyone to dinner tonight.

My parent's Swedish cook and maids are in the kitchen preparing a traditional Swedish Christmas Eve dinner of roast goose and all that accompanies it.

In the living room is a huge spruce alight with a hundred candles. The whole house is redolent with holiday fragrances, the food scents wafting in from the kitchen, the wood smoke from the three fire places, the pine wreaths and boughs releasing their perfumes.

***

Ah, sentimental reunion time, yes?

This is Hanna, leading the Leipzig complement through the front door. Her cheeks are flushed with the cold, with liquor I'm sure, and with an expression of bemused mischief.

Sabine is next, eyeing us all, and me in particular, warily. Peter Cunningham enters next, eyes darting about until he sees my mother, unleashing what my mother said used to be a seductive smile, but now is a puerile leer.

Only Johann enters with a sweet and amiable dignity. He moves slowly, with his cane in front of him. At the step up, Sabine moves to take his arm, but I beat her to it.

Johann says...

Ah, thank you, Sa...

But then his nostrils tell him different...

Ohhh... Frida... Merry Christmas... and congratulations on your performance Thursday night... I was there, you know, and I heard such excited comments about your dancing.

And congratulations to you. Johann. I heard you're playing that night.

I don't realize what a stupid thing I've said until Hanna says...

Well, eyebrow, if you could distinguish Johann's playing from the rest of the orchestra, he's in big trouble with the maestro.

Everyone laughs congenially, but I am annoyed.

I turn to Johann and say, in a perfect imitation of Hanna's voice...

Well Johann. if you could distinguish my fragrance as you came in the door, from the rest of this gathering, you're in big trouble with... (the problem now is I didn't think through my whole retort because I've already had two glasses of champagne, and even though I'm looking right at Sabine, I don't quite have the nerve to say her name).

I look to Orlando to save me, and he says gallantly and absurdly...

Yes, well, you're in trouble with the maestro of this holiday gathering, but since that's me you're quite forgiven.

He swallows twice and his frog prince jowls seem to consume for the time being any tension left in the air.

But it isn't a relaxed and amiable dinner. There's too much history between and among all of us.

However, it is a very moving moment when Hans and Klaus see Johann for the first time in thirteen years. Johann is slightly confused at first about who they are and I realize that once he was taken from Pelican Reach, Klaus and Hans were rarely talked about.

For her part, Hans seems to have set aside whatever history she and Hanna had as mother and daughter.

There is a particular edge therefore in the words and glances between Hanna, and Hans and Klaus. Hans, sitting next to Klaus, periodically writes out a message for Klaus to read, sometimes privately, sometimes aloud.

However, as the meal progresses, the fineness of the food and the wine we all take refuge in, keeps the edge of all the personalities at bay.

***

During the previous week, each night, the ritual of Orlando, my mother, Klaus, Hans, and I have been to retreat to the luxurious log sauna back in the woods away from the house.

Around midnight, Hans writes out a note for Klaus to read at the table...

Let's steam hot for heaven or hell.

Klaus interprets for those who are puzzled...

Hans suggests we all take a sauna, and I guess she wonders how it will be for all of us to be together out there.

***

We traipse across the beaten snow toward the soft glowing light of the sauna lodge. A hired man has kept it warm and lit all evening.

We settle into the various levels of cedar benches, all of us essentially naked, with a white bath towel here and there for those who want one. Only Sabine is making an attempt at modesty.

Hanna's first comment after looking at me, my mother, Hans, and down at her own breasts is...

We are all in agreement, I see, that it is a night appropriate for the power of the bones.

She is right. There are eight pierced nipples to add to Sabine's unease with this Pelican Reach extended family.

For his part, Johann is sitting quiet, listening to the sounds around him, and literally, it seems, becoming intoxicated with the mix of aromas surrounding him.

And quite a mix it is. Our bodies are all glistening brilliantly in the moist heat and the light of the one oil lamp behind Hans and Klaus.

We take turns walking to the hot stones to pour another pitcher of water over them. This movement stirs the redolence of the room each time into one more unique combination of body scent.

When Hans limps past Johann to do her turn at pouring, Johann seems puzzled, and removed from the room.

Klaus follows Hans's movements later, and now Johann is bent over, holding himself in what seems like a small ball of body.

He is crying... whimpering really... and then he leans forward onto the bench above him, which is where I'm sitting, and is two benches below where Klaus and Hans sit.

Johann reaches up with his hands to grip the bench and pulls himself upward with the help of his knees and feet. He is so compact that he seems to have shrunk in size. He kneels on the bench I'm on and reaches out his hand toward Klaus, making small animal sounds.

We are all now staring at Johann, in our heat-drugged state. No one says a word.

Klaus is looking hard at Johann and frowning. Then he reaches out for Johann's hand and pulls him up onto the bench between him and Hans, and in the process, Johann's foot is momentarily on my thigh, and looking down, I'm puzzled to see there is pale thin webbing between his spread toes.

His whimpers are more urgent, and looking up, I see Hans smiling dreamily at Johann, a long stream of drool hanging from her lip.

She pulls Johann to her, and Johann presses his nose into Hans's neck and against her face. Hans then gently turns Johann toward Klaus and urges him in that direction.

Klaus embraces Johann and pulls him to his chest. Johann is now letting out little howls and rubbing his nose and face back and forth across Klaus's cheek and neck.

Klaus in turn hands Johann back into Hans's arms.

This passing of Johann back and forth continues for several minutes and none of us has moved or spoken.

Even Hanna is entranced. Sabine seems in a state of shock.

Now Johann's head seems to be wobbling as though he can barely hold it upright, and he periodically turns his head jerkily toward Klaus's face or Hans's face, squinting.

Klaus now reaches for the oil lamp and holds it next to his face while Johann moves his face close, his eyes inches from Klaus's.

Klaus breaks the silence. Johann is looking at me.

***

It is a month since the mysterious night in my parent's sauna. By the following day, it was clear that Johann could not cope with the emotional and physiological trauma of his suddenly restored vision.

Orlando arranged for him to be taken to a convalescent clinic, an exclusive one where Johann could gradually adjust to the use of his eyes and adjust to all the new faces in his life.

***

The doctors say he will be fine, and he is due to leave the clinic in another week.

Once the excitement of Johann's vision returning has settled in my mind, my thoughts turn from his eyes to his feet. I can't begin to consider the implications of the delicate webbing. I could have been looking at my own feet, just a bit bigger.

***

I told my father what I had seen. Orlando and I were alone in the library, and I watched him silently while his frog prince jowls filled and deflated as he digested my information. He was stunned by what I told him.

Finally, after a long silence, I said...

How could this be, father. Silence.

What does it mean? I can ask Hanna what it means, you know.

At the mention of Hanna's name, Orlando turns to me, his great eyes brimming with distress. Still he is silent.

So, to unlock his archive of Pelican Reach history, I say... You know, father, mother has told me about her affair with Peter Cunningham, eighteen years ago... She told you about that?

Yes.

Silence.

What about you and Hanna, father?

The pain on Orlando's face makes my heart ache. Finally, he speaks...

I wanted to spare you the information about your mother and Peter Cunningham, but that information is linked to what I'm going to tell you about Hanna and me.

But first, let me say that this business of Johann's webbed feet... this is the first I've heard of it. My God!

***

When your mother had her affair with Peter Cunningham, it was essentially a matter of physical infatuation. Peter was not then what he is now, and I would add, that Hanna was not what she is now. It probably seems unbelievable that all of this happened, when you look at Peter and Hanna today. No, father, I have seen photographs of both Hanna and Peter from that time. They were fascinating and beautiful.

I say this to help loosen Orlando's reticence, and it does. Your mother was overwhelmed with sexual attraction to Peter. You see, she had loved and had expected to marry Peter's twin brother, who died suddenly.

At the same time that Peter and your mother were having their intimacy, Peter and Hanna were also together. When Hanna learned about your mother and Peter, she was enraged.

She came to tell me, but I already knew. To me it was obvious. And when Hanna saw that I already knew and she couldn't provoke me into some kind of action, she devised her own retribution.

Even after all these years, it is so embarrassing to characterize my behavior back then. You'll have to fill in with your imagination. Let me just say that her strategy was to use sex with me to eclipse what Peter was doing with your mother.

Her approach to me was so animalistically erotic that she provoked in me a response as base as her own... as lascivious... as obsessive.

Her motives had nothing to do with me personally. On the contrary, it was just an extension of her rage at your mother, and at Peter, but I was too overwhelmed by it to make those distinctions then.

Orlando stops now, I think a little surprised at how much he has told me, and the fervor with which he has told it.

There is a long silence, during which I've taken his hand to show not only that I don't judge him, but that I sympathize with him.

Finally, he speaks softly...

But this business of Johann's feet... my God, Frida, he could be your brother.

Hearing these words finally spoken sends a chill through my body. I have not said them even to myself.

***

When I later talk to my mother, she says...

Yes Frida. It's all true, I'm sorry to say. Like all of life, there's a reason for it... we just don't know yet what the reason is.

Mother is sitting before me in the other rocking chair in her Stockholm studio. We are like photographic negatives of each other... I am as light as she is dark. Our only common feature is our dark wing of an eyebrow.

She has been painting my portrait while she's here... she rarely stays for more than a few weeks. The winters are too Germanic, she says.

I understand that she means it in reference to Hanna, and I reply...

And the Germans are too wintery, Mama.

She laughs, but I don't know yet just how wintery.

***

What still puzzled me though was, since Hanna surely had noticed Johann's webbed feet, with all of her vindictiveness, why did she not flaunt it to my mother and father?

When I ask Orlando about this, he says...

I'm sure she kept it a secret because she knew I would have used all the legal power I have access to take Johann away from her to live with us.

And when I asked Klaus, before he left to return to California, why he and Hans, after they saw Johann's toes, didn't say something, Klaus said...

We wanted to protect your mother from knowing. And, for selfish reasons... you know Hans and Johann and I lived together in the Klaruk village for four years... we loved Johann and wanted him part of our little family. After all, we had a Klaruk ceremony adopting him.

So everyone now knows that Orlando and Johann are father and son... everyone but Johann.

Four months ago, in Leipzig, when I first located Johann and then stayed for those two weeks in his family's fancy mansion... the night when he came to my room and asked to feel my sandpiper bones, and subsequently asked if he could put them in, here's what happened...

My shyness, and my sense of propriety, which ordinarily would have kept me from permitting such a thing, they were shunted aside by great grandmother Kahlo, and her very words were...

What is this, are you just going to hand him over to this little Sabine thing?

So when Johann asked if he could put the bones in (a fairly brazen act for this polite boy, I realized after), I agreed.

I pulled off my dress, and that was safe, since he couldn't see anything, but that was what first aroused me, standing naked in front of him.

I told him he had to use saliva, and I stood there trembling while he settled a little spit on the tip of his finger and pointed it out toward me.

I took his hand and guided it to me, watching with fascination his blind face assimilating everything with his other senses.

His innocence made him seem sweet and endearing.

Because he couldn't see, it took an excruciating amount of fumbling, stretching, inserting, and twisting before he had the bones in place, during which we were both panting so loudly I thought everyone in the house must be listening.

There was of course, no turning back after that, and I had sex for the first time in my life, on the floor with this sweet blind boy, Johann.

When I arrive at the clinic to bring Johann back to our Swedish country house, Johann says after kissing me...

Frida, it's obvious you are harboring some important news inside this sweet head of yours. What is it? I'll just blurt it out.

Orlando is your father.

Johann looks puzzled and bemused, but after I have told him everything, he says...

So, I'm not the son of a murderous East German Berlin Wall guard... isn't that wonderful news, Frida? And I am the son of saintly Orlando... isn't that even more wonderful news, Frida? Somewhat makes up for my mother, doesn't it?

And isn't it even more wonderful still that you and I are brother and sister, Frida. Sabine will be so pleased. You know, she was quite jealous of us.

I stare at Johann in stunned silence with a tear streaming down my cheek.

But Johann, what about the night you came to my room in Leipzig, and put in my bones, and then...

Johann smiles, his eyes on mine alert and sparkling, as though all of life is just beginning to unfold before him.

It was so exciting, wasn't it Frida? You know, from the time I was about ten, my mother talked about the thrill of just that kind of sudden, unpremeditated pleasure.

And the day after I put your bones in, when I told Hanna all that happened, she was so pleased, and said...

It's important, Johann, to take what you want in life.

And it was the same for you, wasn't it Frida? You were taking what you wanted from me... it was completely mutual, wasn't it, dear sister?

***

As we drove back in the taxi from the clinic to my parent's house, I thought about these words of Johann's, which even though they came out of his mouth, seemed to be the words of another person.

I studied Johann, and in his new self-possessed profile, I could see the presence of Hanna.

The presence of Orlando in Johann seemed to dissolve when he regained his vision, and it occurs to me that it was the sensitive and vulnerable frog prince quality of Johann's blindness that I loved.

When we arrive at the house, and I see that mother and Orlando are not home, great grandmother Kahlo invites herself into this quiet afternoon.

What she has in mind is palpably clear (there is a warmth descending the inside of my thigh).

Why, is another matter, and that I understand only later.

Six

It is five years and seven months since I brought Johann home from the clinic, to my parents' Stockholm house, where we made love for the second and last time.

***

I am at Pelican Reach, walking along the damp sand at low tide.

Ahead of me are my five-year-old twins, Frida and Johann, chasing the feeding sandpipers and squealing with delight.

Both arc winged and webbed in the classic Frida/frog prince manner.

Frida is light and Johann is dark, small perfect replicas of their parents.

***

I now dance with the San Francisco Ballet. When I travel, the twins stay with mother and Orlando, a mutually agreeable arrangement.

Johann is in Germany.

He is blind, and he is in prison.

***

Five years ago, when Johann left Stockholm and returned to Leipzig, his future seemed certain. He was to marry Sabine within a month. Hanna bought them an elegant house nearby. His playing reached a new level of facility and beauty, and he was to solo soon with the orchestra.

Hanna spent more and more time with Johann. She was excited about his recovered vision, and constantly asked that he tell her how she looked.

As the wedding date approached, she began to criticize Sabine, using herself as the standard for behavior and appearance. She became increasingly agitated.

Johann became depressed and unsure of what he was doing. He asked that the wedding be postponed.

Finally, one night he went to Hanna's room to tell her that he was going to leave Germany, that he needed to be alone, that he was confused.

Hanna was at first angry, then became elated.

Of course, you're confused, Johann. I'm the one you've always wanted... isn't that true, dearest Johann?

Hanna began to take off her clothes, smiling lasciviously.

Johann had a sudden sense of the serious derangement of his mother, but he was unable to move. He found himself staring at Hanna's obese, indulgent body, creased with angry red underwear lines.

When she approached him, he still couldn't move. He knew he could never move... never get away from Hanna.

The sight of her body was suddenly more than he could take, and some primordial trigger simply stopped the sight... his sight.

He stood still, blind and agonized, until he felt her flesh press against him, and then something else was triggered... a blind rage (literally), and a compulsion to protect himself.

Two days later Johann was in prison. He remembered nothing after he lost his vision. He was told by the police that he had strangled his mother.

I have visited Johann several times over the past five years. He is in prison for life, but as he said...

What difference does it make? I was a prisoner of Hanna's for life.

***

In his blindness, Johann has reverted to the quiet, reflective, and vulnerable presence of his father (and mine), sweet Orlando.

I often ask, who is Johann?... or who was Johann when he was not what he is now? And more important, who was he when making love to me when I conceived my (our) perfectly healthy twins, the night he came to my room in Leipzig, and in his blindness, fumbled with my sandpiper bones and then genuinely loved me and planted the seed of our twins.

All of that was done by Johann outside of Hanna's power. That, I believe is why our twins are normal, even though Johann is my half-brother.

And when I brought Johann home from the clinic, and great grandmother Kahlo urged me into bed with him, her message was... even the score, take your pleasure, realize there's a time for carnality and a time for conception, and the two are unrelated.

I didn't know at the time that I had already conceived, and I have wondered since, if I had conceived then, with Johann in his sighted, Hanna-mode, what the result might have been.

***

The two most haunting things Johann has said to me came in our first prison visit and in our last prison visit.

When he told me about his last lethal moments with his mother, he said...

You know Frida, I'll never know for sure because I couldn't see, but it sounded as though once my hands were around her neck, Hanna was laughing jubilantly.

And the last thing Johann said to me at our last visit was...

You know Frida, I never had a chance... from the moment I was forced into the world from her Satanic womb.

***

Klaus and Hans have moved to Leipzig to be close to Johann.

Hans is writing, in her cryptic poetry, her account of the four years she and Klaus and Johann were a family living with the Klaruk Indians.

These pages, which she sends to Johann daily, are written on the paper made by Klaus, which is more beautiful than ever. They are read to Johann by the prison chaplain.

Hans has also written to Johann that she knows she can restore his vision with her music, but he has begged her not to. He does not want to see what's around him his whole life now is in his mind.

Hans does, however, stand outside the prison, below where she knows Johann's cell is, and plays a dawn improvisation every morning. Johann has said it's the only time when the prison din dissolves, and Hans's notes float through the bleak concrete and steel hallways, and the inmates... the most hardened men on earth... stand silent and motionless in their living prison death while Hans's paean to life pours into them.

***

Johann, also in our last visit said...

I often wonder too, if Hanna ever had a chance.

***

Once Klaus and Hans moved to Leipzig, Johann prodded them relentlessly for information about his mother.

He recites for me his new-found litany of the history of Hanna...

I picture the hard scars from Heinrich Stoller's bullets, as she went over the wall that separated forever who she might have been, from who she became.

I think of her twin brother, Hans, who fucked her, and I think of dear Hans, the product of that sordid liaison, who was intended to be her brother's namesake and stand-in in real life, and who is the only real mother I've ever had, in spite of the fact that she's my sister.

I think of Hanna's attempt to murder Klaus, who then was to become her lover.

I think of her sex with the gardener, who then was revealed to be her attempted murderer.

I think of the killing of that gardener at the hands of Hans, surely an extension of Hanna's power.

I think of Hanna's vengeful seduction of our father, Orlando, which unfortunately resulted in my own birth.

I think of how close love is to hate, and birth is to death. It's all very fleeting, isn't it, dear sister Frida... dear wife,

Frida... you know, that's what you are in my imagination... the only world I live in now... and I think of us all together at Pelican Reach as a family, with our twins and the sandpipers...

***

Those were Johann's last words at our last visit. I don't think I'll go back again.

***

Mommy!

I am above the bank of the river, and the delicate, bell-voice of Frida V is carried up the grassy slope to call my attention to the six pelicans circling my dear family below.

The sun is reflected on the water behind them, and it's like a magic lantern show of a hundred years ago.

Each player has a dual role.

Little Frida and Johann are holding hands and squinting up at me, and they go from themselves to their parents at the age of five, and then back again to themselves.

Orlando has his hand up in a suspended wave, and momentarily he is Diego Rivera, before becoming Orlando again. And my dear mother, looking up with her burning dark eyes below her dark wing, and her impish mouth in a little smile of love, is abruptly magisterial great grandmother Kahlo... or, more accurately, her self-portrait with reflected sunlight shining through the canvas to assert the aliveness of her art as well as herself.

She returns to the presence of my very alive mother, who has her hand up in a suspended wave, as though she and Orlando are a double self-portrait.

***

The feelings flooding me arrive with the force of the tidal flow into the river below.

I flounder in an attempt to find the right words to serve these emotions.

Finally, all I come up with is...

I am Frida Kahlo.

***

And when I say this, I say it three more times, once for each of us, and in each case it's a ringing truth.

***

Then I slip and slide crazily in a giggling descent to the bank of the river where my family waits, laughing with me, all holding out their arms to keep me from plunging past them and into the surging waters.

HISTRIA

BOOKS

HISTRIA FICTION

Other fine books available from Histria Fiction:

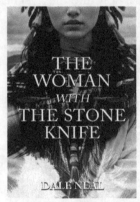
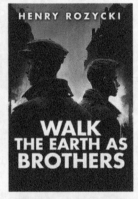
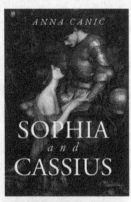
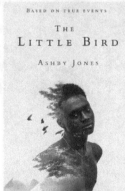
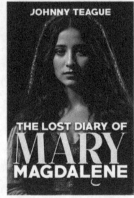

For these and many other great books visit

HistriaBooks.com